"Ah, Glenda, you disappoint me."

The scoffing note in his voice deepened. "I was so sure you would remember everything I ever said to you all those years ago. You were just the tiniest bit in love with me then, and a woman in love always remembers everything a lover says to her," he added softly.

"We weren't lovers in Montreal," she protested. "Have you forgotten I was engaged then. I wasn't the least interested in having you for a lover."

"So why don't you wear a wedding ring?" He shot the question at her.

"Why don't you?" she countered.

She leaned toward him, her face illuminated by the candlelight. He reached across the table to touch her hand, his eyes seeming to smolder. Never before in the whole of her life had she felt desire pulse through her so strongly....

FLORA KIDD had a romantic dream—to own a sailboat and learn how to sail it. That dream came true when she found romance of another sort with a man who shared her love of the sea and became her husband and father of their four children. A native of Scotland, this bestselling romance author now lives in New Brunswick, one of Canada's maritime provinces, with the sea on her doorstep.

Books by Flora Kidd

FLORA KIDD

beloved deceiver

Harlequin Books

TORONTO • NEW YORK • LONDON
AMSTERDAM • PARIS • SYDNEY • HAMBURG
STOCKHOLM • ATHENS • TOKYO • MILAN

Harlequin Presents first edition March 1988
ISBN 0-373-11058-8

Original hardcover edition published in 1987
by Mills & Boon Limited

CHAPTER ONE

GLENDA Thompson stood in front of a table covered with a white cloth. On the cloth, silver and amber pendants winked and glowed. She held one of the pendants in her hand and studied it. The table was one of many lining the entrance to the modern building of the market in Puerto Plata.

People of all sorts and sizes swarmed past the table, some bumping against Glenda as she concentrated on the amber stone in the palm of her hand. Many voices clamoured in her ears and she had to lean close to the proprietress of the jewellery stall to hear the plump, dusky-skinned, black-eyed woman tell her the price of the pendant in *pesos*.

Mentally she changed the amount of *pesos* into Canadian dollars. Twenty dollars. She wondered whether she should attempt to bargain with the stall owner. The silver chain sliding over her fingers, she held the stone up, turning away from the stall to study the amber against the light shafting in through the opening of the market hall. Amber was well named the 'burning-stone', she thought. Not only could it really be burnt because it was a fossil resin, but it also looked as if it was on fire when light shone through it.

A movement in the slow-moving crowd of shoppers drew her attention away from the burning-stone that was dangling from her fingers. Through the spaces between her spread-out fingers she saw him, the man she had been trying to see ever since she had arrived in the Dominican Republic. He was tall and was dressed in white slacks and a white shirt decorated with embroidery on either side of its slit opening. His hair was an unusual colour, sand-coloured, thick, springing up from his head in wiry curls, contrasting strangely with his darkly tanned skin. It was that hair that made him recognisable to her. He was César Estrada, no doubt about that.

There was nothing wrong with Glenda's reflexes. Determined to follow him now that she had seen him at last, she dropped the pendant on the table, slung the handles of her big canvas shopping bag over one shoulder and, ignoring the strident protests of the stall proprietress, she set off in pursuit of César, dodging between the tourists and local people, always keeping in view that proud head of sand-coloured hair, glad that he wasn't wearing his hat but was carrying it in one hand. It wasn't the first time she had chased a person in the course of her career as a freelance writer of articles about interesting celebrities.

Inside the main building of the market, nothing was orderly. Fruit and vegetables, brought in from the country that morning, spilled over from baskets and boxes. Ripe oval tomatoes, brown mangoes, scarlet peppers, yellow bananas, crates of golden-brown eggs, and pineapples, huge, huge pineapples.

It was a pineapple that stopped Glenda in her tracks as she was rounding a curve. Held out to her on the palm of a hand of a little man with a wizened face the colour of a walnut, it was offered to her for only half a *peso*. Not quite ripe, its yellow diamond-shaped facets slightly tinged with green, it tempted her. She thought of how it would taste when it was fully ripe and her mouth watered. Acting on impulse, she agreed to buy it. Beyond the little man, at the next stall, she had spotted her quarry, César Estrada, who was also buying fruit.

While she searched her mind for ways to approach César, she absentmindedly agreed to buy everything the little man offered her, keeping her eyes on César, afraid he might go off without her seeing in which direction he went. It wasn't until a big brown paper bag was thrust at her that she realised how much fruit she had agreed to buy. His sharp black eyes twinkling at her, the little man demanded six *pesos*.

Ruefully amused at her own extravagance in allowing herself to be persuaded to buy four pounds of tomatoes, twenty bananas, several peppers and six oranges, as well as the pineapple, and wondering what she was going to do with all of them when she got back to the hotel where she was staying, Glenda looked in her handbag for the wallet in which she kept her foreign currency. Six *pesos* wasn't much, possibly less than two Canadian dollars, but she didn't really need all that much fruit.

She groped and groped. There was no hard comforting square of leather. Alarmed, she swung her shopping bag to the floor, pulled out her handbag and peered into it. The plain black leather wallet was missing. She was still staring into the handbag when she heard the fruit-seller questioning her in Spanish. She looked at him, her own Spanish deserting her completely in that moment of distress.

'I have no money, 'she said.' I have lost my wallet.'

The fruit-seller, it seemed, knew enough English to understand what she had said. His voice rising angrily, he pushed the bulging bag of fruit at her and demanded his six *pesos*.

'*No tengo dinero, señor*. I have no money.' Glenda spoke loudly and slowly.' I have lost my wallet. I cannot pay you right now.'

The little man seemed to go beserk. He ranted and raved at her, calling to passers-by to come and see this terrible *gringa* woman who had chosen fruit for which she couldn't pay.

Embarrassed by the fuss he was making and anxious about the loss of her wallet, Glenda attempted to apologise to him, aware that a disapproving group of people had stopped to stand and stare at the little man's passionate performance.

'Excuse me. Perhaps I can help you.'

César Estrada was beside her, offering his help in a deep warm voice that held only the slightest of lilting Spanish accents. She looked up at him in relief. His eyes, the colour of the amber pendant she had so recently held in her hand, glimmered down at her through fringes of black lashes. His face was leaner than when she had last seen him, both cheeks scarred by lines carved by either experience or endurance. His long shapely lips slanted in the slightest of smiles.

'I've mislaid my wallet and I can't pay for the fruit,' she explained, aware of an unusual breathlessness now that she was actually face to face with him again after not seeing him for eight years. All the liking she had felt for him rushed into her mind suddenly, pushing aside all other thoughts for a few seconds. She stared up at him, her feelings expressed, although she didn't know it, in her eyes. He looked back at her, his own eyes narrowing slightly, and for those few seconds they both seemed trapped in a bubble of time, deaf and blind to everything around them, until the shrill voice of the fruit-seller pierced the bubble. César turned to the little man and spoke a few sharp words in Spanish.

Immediately the fruit-seller stopped raving and became quite servile and obsequious. César pushed a hand into a trouser pocket, brought out some *peso* notes and pressed them into the little man's outstretched hand. Then, pulling his broad-brimmed white sunhat aslant on his head, he took the bag containing Glenda's purchases, gathering it into the crook of his left arm. He was already holding a similar bag in the crook of his right arm.

'So—no problem. He is paid,' he said, turning to her with another slight smile. 'Let's go.'

He set off with long-legged strides and she followed. She tried to catch up with him to say her thanks, but every time she got closer to him someone got in her way. But as she dodged through the crowds of shoppers her heart was singing, and not just with triumph because she had at last tracked him down. It was singing because she was so glad to meet him again. Of all the men she had ever known, he was the only one who had ever fascinated her to the point where she would have willingly cast discretion to the winds if only he had ever asked her to go away with him or to live with him. But he never had.

Down the flights of steps leading up to the market building she hurried after him. Heat from the bright sun hit her and she paused, wishing she had brought her sunhat. At the bottom of the steps he waited for her, watching her approach him, and she was glad her legs were a good shape below the hem of her thin, brightly patterned, wraparound cotton skirt.

'Thank you. Thank you very much for paying for the fruit,' she said when she reached him.

'*De nada*. You are most welcome. But about your wallet—do you think you have left it somewhere, at another stall perhaps? Or in a shop in the town?'

'I think I may have left it in my room at the hotel,' she said.' I changed handbags this morning and I could have forgotten to take it from the bag I was using yesterday.'

'Then tell me where your car is and I will carry this bag to it for you,' he said crisply.

'I don't have a car. I walked up from the *plaza*. I came up here because I was told at your house this morning that you'd gone to the market to buy fruit. I came hoping to find you here,' she said, the breathlessness overcoming her again. She felt somewhat dizzy, too. Surely it had nothing to do with meeting him again?

She was unprepared for the unpleasant narrowing of his eyes and the almost sneering curl of his long upper lip. For a brief moment he looked cruelly derisive, then the expression had gone, wiped as if by a sponge from his lean dark face.

'You followed me? 'he asked.' Why?'

'Oh, César, don't you remember me? I'm Glenda Thompson. We used to know each other when you were in Montreal, at Concordia. You were studying for an MA in English and I was studying English, too, for my BA. I've called at your house several times during the past week. I left a message for you . . . '

'Ah.' Comprehension dawned. Within the shadow of his hat-brim his brilliant amber-flecked eyes sparkled with sudden amusement, a devilry that both intrigued and surprised her. 'So you are the woman who has been calling at the old house!'

'You don't remember me, do you?' she accused him. 'You've forgotten me. I know it's been a while since we last met, but I can't have changed all that much. I recognised you as soon as I saw you going by in the market. You weren't wearing your hat then and I recognised you by your hair. It's so different. You told me once that one of your Spanish ancestresses, the wife of another César Estrada who came from Spain to Hispaniola to seek his fortune in the silver mines and stayed to become governor, was ravished by

English pirate and that, every other generation,
his fair hair and lighter eyes appear in your
family.'

'Did I tell you that? How very imaginative of
me,' he remarked, his eyes dancing again with
mischief. 'And to think you've remembered that
tall story of mine all this time! ' He laughed,
white teeth flashing, and she couldn't help but be
infected by his mirth. 'I must have been trying to
make a good impression on you and I must have
succeeded if you've remembered so much.' His
face sobered and he glanced away from her, a
frown between his dark eyebrows. 'It's all coming
back to me now,' he murmured, 'the memory of
those times in Montreal that we had together.
We had fun.' He looked back at her with an
inquiring lift of one eyebrow.

'Yes, we had fun,' she replied. 'And last time
we met you told me that if I ever came to your
country I should look you up, call on you, so
that you could return the hospitality you had
received while you were in Montreal. I'm here on
a week's package holiday, so I've taken the
opportunity to call to see you. I fly back to
Toronto on Sunday.'

'I see.' He studied her face, his bright glance
shifting; warm as the sunlight, it seemed to her,
flicking over her eyes, her cheeks, and down to
her lips, where it lingered a few seconds before
flashing up to her eyes again.

'I find it incredible that you're here, Glenda,
and that we're standing here talking to each other
so far away from Canada after so many years,'
he said softly, his voice as warmly caressing as

his eyes had been. 'I hope you'll excuse me for not remembering you right away; I returned to Puerto Plata only last night. There were many messages for me, I didn't look at all of them properly. You say you're leaving on Sunday? That doesn't give me much time to repay all the kindness and generous hospitality I received in Montreal.'

'It doesn't matter,' Glenda said quickly. 'I don't want you to think I was expecting anything special. I just want to talk to you about your novel. I was so excited when I heard of the award you received for it. I've read it. It's wonderful and I'd like to interview you.'

'Interview?' He spoke sharply, looking at her with unpleasant suspicion again.

'Yes. That's what I do now. I interview interesting people and write articles about them to sell to magazines. I'll be writing one about this country and I thought that, if you would let me interview you, I could write one about you and your novel. It would be of interest to Canadian readers because you were once a post-graduate student at a Canadian university. Would you let me interview you today or tomorrow, or some time before I go back to Toronto?'

She had hardly finished speaking when a faintness swept through her. She saw his face through a wavering haze and she swayed on her feet as sharp pains needled through her stomach. She almost fainted.

'I'm sorry, she muttered, a hand at her forehead, which felt very hot. 'It's the heat, I think. I'm not used to it.'

She thought the quick glance he gave her was sceptical and that he didn't believe in her faintness, but in the next instant she discarded the thought because he put down the two bags of fruit on a step and, taking hold of her arm, urged her towards them, pushing her down to sit on the step.

'Wait here, 'he ordered, his voice crisp with authority. 'I'll go and get my truck. I'll drive you back to your hotel.'

He strode away. Taking out a handkerchief, Glenda wafted it in front of her face, trying to create a cool draught. She felt feverishly hot one moment, shiveringly cool the next. She became aware that a group of people had collected about her. A young woman in a brightly coloured dress asked in Spanish-accented English if she was all right. She forced herself to smile and assured the woman she was all right and that she was waiting for a friend.

Suddenly the group was dispersed, seemed to be blown away by a strong wind, and there was César again, his eyes piercingly sharp in the shadow of his hat-brim as he reached out a hand to help her to her feet.

Inside the cab of the small grey Hyundai truck it was stiflingly hot and the seat covering burned through the thin material of her skirt to her thighs. She found a handle and wound down the window on her side. Not much air came in to refresh her, but the noise of the truck and the smell of its exhaust did as it shot away from the steps, turned in a swerving semi-circle and charged out of the parking space into a narrow street.

Down the hill to the *plaza* the truck hurtled, passing old houses with wrought-iron balconies and gingerbread decoration edging their roofs. The *plaza* was busy with traffic, mostly motorcycles ridden by young people. The walls of the twin-towered church gleamed ivory white in the bright sunshine and in the centre of the square's garden, which was ablaze with the crimson and gold of blossoming tropical shrubs, the quaint two storey bandstand was elegant in white paint with a blue trim.

'I'm staying at the Playa Dorada,' said Glenda as the truck shot across an intersection and followed the main shopping street out of the *plaza*. She was relieved that the faintness had passed and, although she felt shaken up and jolted by the ride in the truck, she was beginning to feel more normal. 'And about the interview. You will let me interview you, won't you, César? Please . . . ' She broke off as the truck swerved dangerously to avoid another vehicle which seemed to run out of control from an uphill side street and across their path.

'I didn't know you could drive,' she gasped, looking around for the seatbelt, grabbing it and buckling it quickly. 'I mean, you never drove in Montreal.' Secretly she thought it was just as well he hadn't. Quebec drivers were considered the most reckless and aggressive in Canada, but they had nothing on Dominicans.

'That was because I didn't own a car,' he replied, flashing her a sidelong glance. 'You're feeling beter now?'

'Yes, thank you. Much better,' she lied. Nausea

and faintness weren't bothering her any more,
but his driving was.

'What would you put in the article?' he asked.

'That would depend on how you answered my
questions. I'd concentrate on your background
and education here in the Dominican Republic,
and would then go on to ask you about the
philosophy that lies behind the story in your
novel and why you decided to write it in English
rather than in Spanish.'

'And where would you want to interview me?'
he asked.

'At your house, perhaps this afternoon?'

'That is impossible.'

'Tomorrow, then. In the morning. I always
work better in the mornings, especially in this
tropical climate.'

'I won't be in town tomorrow,' he replied.
'Right now I'm going to Samana. Why don't you
come with me and allow me to return the Canadian hospitality I once enjoyed?'

'Isn't Samana a long way from here?' she
demurred, although she had every intention of
accepting his invitation.

'We could be there soon after one o'clock,' he
said. 'In time for *siesta*.' He flashed her another
glance. 'Will you come? It's the only way you'll
get your interview with me. I own a house there,
by the sea. You'll like it; it has its own beach,
the swimming is wonderful, the views magnificent, the peace and privacy perfect.'

'I'd love to come, but I'll have to go to the
hotel first to see if I've left my wallet there. It
isn't the wallet I keep my dollars and travellers'

cheques in—it contains only *pesos*—but I'd like to make sure I've mislaid it through my own absentmindedness and that it hasn't been stolen.'

'No problem. I understand,' he replied. 'And while you're at the hotel you can pick up a swimsuit, a change of clothes and some night-wear.' He sent her another glance. 'You'll stay the night with me, Glenda? Maybe two nights? If you stay I'll bring you back to the hotel in time for you to check out on Sunday morning and to catch the flight back to Canada.'

She glanced at him in surprise. Was he making a pass at her by suggesting that she should stay the night with him, maybe two nights? Or was it just his way of issuing an invitation? He had never made a serious pass at her when she had known him in Montreal. Never once had they slept together, but she had to admit that she had secretly wished they had.

Already she had noticed differences in him: a hard edge, a sharp arrogance that hadn't been there when she had known him in Montreal. True, he was eight years older, possibly thirty-six now, and he had some achievement behind him: a wonderful novel that was an international success and had been awarded an American literary prize.

And, too, here in this beautiful tropical country of high mountains, deep valleys, wide plains, of coconut farms and sugar plantations, he was on his own ground, in his own climate. Climate, she had read, influenced a person's behaviour. Possibly when he had lived in the colder climate of Montreal during the freezing winter he had behaved differently from the way he behaved when he lived here.

She glanced sideways at him, her eyes taking a swift photographic shot of his dark profile below the hat-brim. High-bridged Spanish nose, firm lips, clean-cut angular jaw. From his profile her glance leapt to the lean tanned hands on the steering wheel and from them to the long thigh shaping the thin cotton of his slacks. Was her memory playing tricks on her? Hadn't he been slightly fatter when she had known him in Montreal? She was sure there had been times when he had seemed fatter than he was now. Perhaps clothes made a difference. Here, he had to wear very little.

'So, Glenda, will you come to Samana with me?' he queried.

'I'd like to. Will there be anyone else at the house?'

'*Si,* there will be someone else there, 'he replied coolly.

'Your wife?' she asked. 'I heard you were married. Do you have children?'

'We will not discuss my marriage,' he snapped. 'Not now or at any other time. No questions, please, about that when you interview me.'

'All right,' said Glenda stiffly, feeling rebuffed. 'I have no intention of prying into your private life; I was just showing a friendly interest. We were friends once and used to talk a lot to each other.' She paused, remembering those times when they had seemed closest, when she had felt she could have talked to him for ever, sharing dreams and hopes. 'Remember the time we went down to my parents' place in the Eastern Townships, just before you left Montreal?' she said softly. 'And the fun we had sailing my brother's dinghy on the lake? When they heard I was going to look for you, Mum and Dad asked me to remember them to you. They sent their best wishes to you and congratulations on the success of your book.'

César didn't answer, and for once seemed to be concentrating on driving carefully along the narrow road that wound about clumps of palms and casuarinas. The road ended in a courtyard in front of a long low building with a roof of thatched palm leaves. It was the main building of the hotel complex and housed the dining-room, lounge, bar, offices and kitchen. Guests stayed in individual thatched huts which were scattered among the plantation of palms edging the wide spectacular beach of pale golden sand. Beyond the beach stretched the sea, endlessly it seemed, turquoise and emerald, glittering with silver sparks of light under the blazing sun. Long breakers tumbled and broke in bursts of sparkling foam on the sand.

'I will wait for you here,' said César as he parked the truck under the drooping fronds of some palms near the main building. He turned to her. His smile was as warm as the sunlight, flitting across the dark planes and angles of his face. 'And your parents' good wishes and congratulations are most welcome. It's good to be remembered by such kind people and I hope your short stay with me at Samana will, in a small way, repay their hospitality to me during those few days I stayed at Orford.'

Although very formal, the result perhaps of
him having thought through what he wanted to
say to her in Spanish before saying it in English,
his acknowledgment of her parents' message had
the effect of smothering the strange anxious feeling
that had been growing inside her ever since he
had snubbed her over the matter of his marriage.
Once again he was as she had remembered; polite,
friendly and appreciative. She smiled back at him.

'I won't be long,' she said, and opened the
door beside her. As she walked through the trees
to the hut she was sharing with her friend, Ida
Katin, another writer who worked for an adver-
tising agency, Glenda felt her head throb again.
There was a slight queasiness in her stomach,
too. She hoped she hadn't got sunstroke or picked
up some tropical bug. She supposed she shouldn't
go with César to Samana if there was any possibility of her being ill; she ought to stay at the
hotel and rest until she felt better.

But the chance to interview him wouldn't come
again, she felt sure of that. Anyway, she wanted
to go with him. Meeting him again had revived
the strong attraction she had felt towards him.
She had liked him very much when she had
known him Montreal and if she hadn't been so
involved with Greg at the time, if she hadn't
promised to marry Greg, she might have . . .

With a shake of her head she banished such
thoughts and, stepping on to the veranda of the
hut, opened the door. The big bed-sitting-room
had been cleaned and tidied. Both single beds
were neat and smooth and there was a strong

smell of disinfectant coming from the bathroom. Ida wasn't there and Glenda guessed her friend was on the beach either sunbathing or playing volley ball with some of the other tourists.

She went straight to the wardrobe and took out her suitcase. Heaving it on to her bed, she unlocked it and opened it; inside was her red handbag. A quick search of the bag brought to light the wallet containing the *pesos,* and she breathed a sigh of relief. No need now to report its loss to the police. She transferred the wallet to her other handbag, locked the suitcase again, and put it back in the wardrobe.

Quickly she found her swimsuit, a towel and her beach robe. She rolled them up and put them in her canvas shopping bag on top of her tape-recorder and camera. She decided not to take any nightwear or a change of clothing, as César had suggested, because she hoped to persuade him to drive her back to the hotel later in the day. It wouldn't be wise to stay with him for the night if he was still married.

She wrote a note for Ida explaining that she had at last found César Estrada and was going to Samana with him, but would be back, if not that evening then some time the next day. She propped the note against Ida's cosmetic case on the chest of drawers and then considered her own appearance in the long mirror on the wardrobe door.

Her dark brown hair, which she wore in a shoulder-length bob, was smooth and shining, her oval face was lightly tanned to a becoming golden-pink and the lime-green blouse with the scooped-out neckline accentuated the green flecks in her round, heavy-lidded Irish grey eyes. Her headache seemed to have gone. Smiling to herself, feeling a soaring lift of her spirits because she had at last met César again and was going to interview him, have his company for at least the rest of the day, she put on her sunhat and her sunglasses and, picking up her shopping bag, left the hut.

CHAPTER TWO

CÉSAR was leaning against the door of the truck, hat tilted forward over his eyes, arms folded across his chest, ankles crossed casually. To Glenda's surprise smoke drifted upwards from a cigar he held between his teeth.

'I didn't know you smoked,' she said bluntly.

'I don't often, and only when I'm here, at home,' he replied, removing the cigar from his mouth. Within the shadow of the hat-brim his eyes glinted wickedly. 'Dominican cigars rival Cuban cigars,' he told her. 'We foster a sin economy in this island—rum, tobacco and coffee. All offensive, I've no doubt, to a northern puritan like yourself.' His glance slanted down at her canvas bag and he frowned. 'Do you have all you need in that bag?'

'Yes.'

'Then give it to me. I'll put it on the back of the truck to give us more room in the cab. What would you like to do with your fruit?' Again his eyes mocked her. 'You bought far too much for one person; enough to last a Dominican family for a week. Why did you buy so much?'

'I meant only to buy the pineapple, but then I saw you at the next stall and I was so busy watching you, afraid you might move on before I could speak to you, that I must have agreed to buy everything the fruit-seller offered me,' she explained.

'And then you put on that act to draw my attention, I suppose,' he remarked drily. 'Pretending you didn't have enough money to pay him.'

'I wasn't pretending,' she retorted. 'How can you think I'd play such a trick?'

He laughed at her and she felt again that sudden surge of attraction to him. He had liked to tease her, she remembered.

'You still rise easily to a bait,' he mocked. 'And I love the way your eyes flash and your cheeks go pink whenever you feel affronted. Shall we take your fruit with us? If you don't need it I know of a family who'll be glad of it.'

'Then I'd be glad for them to have it,' she said. 'And now I can pay you what I owe you. My wallet was in my other handbag. Here you are.' She offered him some *pesos* and with a shrug of his shoulders he took them and stuffed them in his pocket. He heaved her bag into the back of the truck, then opened a door and gestured to her to get into the cab.

She was glad he put out his cigar before switching on the engine of the truck. She didn't think she could have put up with the smell of the smoke in the small hot cab. He drove back to the highway and soon they were speeding east along the smooth tarmac.

Ahead of them the road delved into steep hills blanketed with the ubiquitous coconut palms. Straight trunks and down-curving fronds shimmered hazily in the sunlight. At the side of the

road thatched huts appeared, simple affairs, no
more than shacks really, squatting amongst the
dense undergrowth. Where there were clearings,
brown-skinned children played, and occasionally
a woman, her head bound in a bright kerchief or
shaded by a straw hat, waved a friendly greeting
at the truck.

After a few miles they reached a village and
swung past a small church, with a red-painted tin
roof and a tiny belfry, on to a narrower rougher
road. White crosses and headstones gleamed
among the long grasses of the graveyard, which
was shaded by two huge trees, poincianas, their
scarlet blossoms seeming to ignite the blue sky
with flames. Beyond the graveyard, some straw-
hatted men sat around on the steps of a shack-
like general store, while a big sign advertised the
local rum, Bermudez.

The narrow road climbed on in a series of
switchback bends up the side of a hill.

'I've come this way to show you something of
the countryside of the Samana peninsula,'
explained César. 'You might find it interesting if
you're going to write an article about this country.
The highway we've just left goes to the head of
Samana Bay and on along the coast to the port
of Santa Barbara de Samana. This road keeps to
the ocean side of the peninsula before crossing
the mountains to the bay. There are views of the
Caribbean Sea and many coconut farms this
way.'

As the truck lurched from pothole to pothole
and often seemed to hang over the edges of steep-
sided valleys, Glenda couldn't help wishing he

hadn't chosen to show her the farms or the views
of deep blue valleys slashing through hills covered
with green rain forests. Sometimes she felt she
was in a car on a roller-coaster as the truck
crawled up the side of one hill, only to rush at
an unnerving breakneck speed down the other
side.

The painful throb in her head started up again
until her whole head felt many sizes larger than
usual. Several times her stomach leapt up as if it
wanted to leave her body altogether. She tried
hard to listen to what César was telling her about
the farms, how big they were, how much coconut
oil each one produced, how irrigation had been
improved a few years ago to help with the culti-
vation of the peninsula. She knew he was doing
it to inform her of the history and development
of his country, as once she had informed him
about the area in the province of Quebec where
her family had settled long ago and where she
had grown up, so she made an effort to ask
suitable questions.

'You will find many people speak English as
their first language, here in Samana,' he said.
'They are descendants of American slaves and
freedmen who were helped to escape from the
States by abolitionists of slavery. They came in
about the year 1824. That was when the whole
of the island of Hispaniola was under Haitian
domination. You'll find families with names like
Brown, Green, Shepherd and even Thompson.'

'How long were the Haitians in control?'
Glenda asked.

'From 1822 until 1844. They emancipated the

Dominican slaves, but their régime was often cruel and despotic. The 'father of our country', Juan Pablo Duarte, drove them out and established the Dominican Republic, independent of both Spain and Haiti. In turn he was driven out and another constitution was written.' He laughed wryly. 'We have had twenty-eight other constitutions since then, most of them administered by despots until recently. Now, thanks to economic aid from the States, Canada and other countries, we make slow progress. But we still have problems; a high birthrate, malnutrition, power and water shortages, racial inequality, diseases. *Por Dios,* there is still much to do to help the poor people . . . ' His voice grated harshly and he broke off.

'The farms look very poor,' remarked Glenda as they passed another cluster of huts with red tin roofs. Hens ran squawking in front of the truck along the narrow road before trying to fly off to the side, and some children dressed in ragged shorts waved and whistled.

'The beauty of the land and the warmth of the climate often tend to soften the shock of the poverty,' said César. 'In this country, as you see, you don't need much in the way of shelter or clothing.' He slanted her a glance. 'Not like your country, where you have to spend much on heating and warm clothing in the winter.'

'That's true,' murmured Glenda, clinging to the rim of the door window beside her as the truck hurtled down what seemed to be the bed of a dried-up river more than a road, there were so many rocks and holes in it.

Up to the crest of yet another hill the truck
climbed, and it hovered there for a few moments.
The land fell away to the left in alternating ridges
and valleys, smothered by the rain forest, a
flowing pattern of different greens fading into a
blue mistiness striped by a long band of silvery
light.

'That is our last glimpse of the ocean. You see
the sunlight shining on the water?' said César. 'A
little further on we'll turn right and go over the
mountain and then you'll see the Bay of Samana.'
He glanced at her as if becoming aware of her
sudden lack of interest. 'Are you feeling all right?'

'A little travel sickness, that's all. This road's a
bit like the big dipper at a fair,' she replied,
managing a smile.

'I'll drive more slowly, then.'

He may have driven more slowly for all she
knew. The rest of the ride was like a wild nightmare for her. A cloud of black hovered just
before her eyes, threatening to cover them
completely. Her head ached and nausea gagged
in her throat. Desperately she clung to the window
rim, fighting off the faintness, determined not to
give in to it. Alternate waves of heat and cold
swept over her and outside the trees and shrubs
went by in a green blur.

Up and down, round and about, the truck
lurched and then suddenly seemed to tumble
down a final rocky bend and on to the highway
that they had left earlier. The sea was blue and
gold on the right, stretching away to distant
purple pointed hills.

'That is the great Bay of Samana,' said César.

'Several Spanish galleons were wrecked in it, caught by hurricanes and driven on to dangerous reefs. They have been explored by divers and much of their treasure is in the museum at Santo Domingo.'

Looking ahead at the distant white buildings of a town, Glenda relaxed a little, sinking back in her seat. Surely now her stomach would settle and the black cloud would lift from her eyes. She closed her eyes but opened them swiftly, wishing she hadn't. For that brief moment she had almost lost control, had almost been sucked down into a deep black abyss.

Down a slope, past a row of stores and a market building, the truck rode, then turned left at a triangle of dusty grass into a wide boulevard. On the right the water of a harbour shimmered blue, protected from the surging waters of the bay by a palm-dotted island. On the left, modern rectangular buildings appeared, creamy white against the green vegetation of the hills at the back of the town.

A stone wharf jutted out into the harbour. Beside it a grey coastal patrol boat was tied up, the Dominican flag—two red and two blue squares divided by a white cross—hanging at its stern. Also tied up to the wharf by their sterns were two big sailing yachts. Both of them, much to Glenda's surprise, were flying Canadian flags. For a few moments she perked up.

'Look, Canadian yachts!' she exclaimed.

'There are often yachts in this harbour, from many different countries. The town is a tourist area and if you look back across the harbour to the headland you'll see a hotel building. It is owned by a Canadian company,' said César.

She made the effort, twisting in her seat and looking out through the open window as the truck followed the boulevard where it curved close to the shoreline of the small protected bay. The headland was high and green and the hotel building was halfway up, white with Spanish-style arches. Below it a pretty bridge connected the palm-dotted island to the mainland.

The boulevard fizzled out and became another country road that twisted and climbed. At last the truck turned off the road and into a narrow lane that slanted straight through a plantation of the inevitable palms and ended in a cleared space beside a low white-walled house with a red-tiled roof. Exotic shrubs and trees crowded about the house: long-leaved sanseveria, prickly cactus, wild poinsettia and spiky-leafed oleanders. At the end of the house, facing the clearing, a wrought-iron staircase slanted up the wall to a veranda built at the front, which faced the sea.

'So here we are,' said César with a note of satisfaction as he parked the car under the shade of casuarina. 'This is my hideaway, where I come to retreat. I hope you'll like it.'

He opened his door and jumped down, slamming the door shut. Wincing at the noise of the slam and wondering vaguely what she was going to do, because the feeling of faintness and nausea, instead of going away, had grown worse, Glenda opened the door on her side and swung her legs out. Slowly she slid off the seat. Below her the sand-coloured earth rippled alarmingly. She seemed to be falling towards it. She was falling after all into the deep black abyss. Just before she reached the bottom she heard a voice exclaim and felt arms go around her. Then she sank downwards and knew no more.

When she came round, she felt she was whirling round and round for a few seconds and that she was very cold. Someone was dripping ice-cold water on to her face. She shivered, gasped and opened her eyes. Her hot dry tongue darted out to lick at drops of water she could feel close to the corners of her mouth. She looked up at a face the colour of bronze topped by sand-coloured hair. Amber-coloured eyes gleamed at her from under level black eyebrows. She was lying on a bed and César was sitting on it beside her, bathing her face with an ice-cold cloth.

'What happened?' she whispered, and watched his lips slant into a sardonic grin.

'Everyone says that when coming out of a faint,' he remarked. 'You fainted as you got out of the truck. Lucky for you I was there. I caught you and brought you in here.' His face hardened. 'Why didn't you tell me you felt ill?'

'I . . . I thought it would pass,' she muttered, then groaned as nausea heaved in her. He stopped bathing her face, tossed the cloth on to a bedside table and looked back at her. She had the impression he was intensely irritated. His eyes were narrow and unsmiling, his lips curled cynically.

'You felt ill at the market, didn't you?' he snapped at her, and she nodded slightly. 'Then why the hell did you agree to come here with me?

Why didn't you say so at the hotel and stay in your cabin?'

'I've told you, I thought it would pass. And I wanted to come with you. I want to interview you,' she retorted weakly.

'You're not pregnant, are you?' was the next snappish question.

'No, of course not!' She was indignant and reared up from the pillows. Immediately the nausea welled up within her. 'Oh, help, I'm going to be sick!' she gasped, and clapped a hand over her mouth.

Somehow she was off the bed and César was beside her, a hand under her elbow half guiding and half pushing her across the room into a passageway and through another doorway into another room. With a sort of hazy relief she saw the toilet, bent over it, lifted the seat and vomited painfully and ignominiously, not caring whether he was watching or not, too ill to care. When she had stopped and was a shaking, retching mess, she felt his hand again on her arm, then his arm about her waist. Supported by him, she got back to the bedroom somehow and lay down thankfully on the bed, closing her eyes and sinking into a feverish stupor.

Several times during the afternoon she had to rush from the bed to the bathroom to be sick again. Sometimes he was with her, sometimes he wasn't. Lying weak and faint on the bed, she was vaguely aware of the light fading and shadows creeping across the bed, then later of the soft glow of lamplight and the bed edge sinking as he sat down beside her again and laid his long cool fingers on her brow.

'I wouldn't have brought you if I'd known you were going to be so ill,' he said softly. 'What have you been doing lately that could have made you so sick? Have you been drinking the water from the taps?'

'No.' Her voice sounded as if it belonged to someone else. 'We drink . . . Ida and I . . . only bottled water. We've tried to be very careful. But I might have had too much sun yesterday. We stood for a long time in line to go up the funicular to the summit of Isabela de Torres. It was very hot.'

His lips thinned and he murmured something in Spanish about her being foolish. Glenda would have liked to have made some retort, but she felt too weak; embarrassed, too, at having been trapped in this situation with him.

'It would be best if you changed into your nightgown,' he suggested curtly, getting up from the bed. 'I will take your skirt and blouse and have them washed.'

'But I didn't bring my nightgown,' she whispered.

'Why not?' Standing by the bed, he seemed to tower over her threateningly. 'I told you to bring your nightwear and a change.'

'I know you did, but I didn't. I had no intention of staying the night here. I hoped you'd drive me back to the hotel.'

'All that way?' His tone was derisive. 'You expected a lot! You see, I had no intention of driving you back.' His breath hissed as he drew it in impatiently. 'So if you have nothing to change into I have to find something for you.' His mouth quirked into a sardonic grin. 'I have to admit that when I invited you to come and stay here I had no idea I would be caring for a sick woman. I had something quite different in mind.'

With that enigmatic statement he turned away and went over to the chest of drawers. Biting her lip, feeling tears of weakness welling in her eyes, Glenda wondered what he had had in mind. He came back to the bed carrying what looked like a white pyjama jacket in one hand. He sat down beside her again and leaned forward to study her face closely, his eyebrows slanting in a frown. She twisted her head sideways on the pillow so that he couldn't see her tears.

'You don't have to care for me—I can manage very well by myself. Just leave me alone. I'll be all right,' she said stiffly.

Against her jaw his fingers were hard. He forced her head round so he could see her face again.

'No, you won't be all right. You have a fever and you're probably going to vomit again. Now let me help you take off your clothes and you can put on this jacket of mine,' he said firmly. 'It should cover you down to your knees.' A laugh shook his voice. 'You'll look very sexy in it. Much good that will do either of us considering the state you're in! Now come on, sit up.'

'No. Please go away. I . . . I'll take off my clothes and put on the jacket, I promise, if you'll just go away,' she whispered.

'OK.' He stood up again, much to her relief, leaving the jacket on the bed.

Without another word he left the room. Glenda heaved herself up into a sitting position. Her head reeled and nausea surged. Somehow she managed to get her blouse off and pull on the pyjama jacket. Made from fine silky cotton, it was far too big for her. She managed to button it up before the nausea surged up again, sending her scurrying unsteadily from the bed across the room, along the passage and into the bathroom. When she returned to the bedroom even more unsteadily she untied her wraparound skirt and let it slip to the floor before she fell on to the bed and succumbed again to the black gulf of feverish exhaustion.

Some time later she was vaguely aware of César beside her making her sit up while he forced her to take some medicine. After taking it she lay hot and dizzy for a while. Slowly the throbbing in her head faded and sweat started on her skin. She felt herself slipping into sleep, and turned on to her side to get into a more comfortable position. To her surprise she found that César was lying on the bed only a short distance away from her. His broad brown back to her, he was wearing only shorts. She spoke to him, but he didn't answer, and while she was wondering blearily why he was there she fell asleep.

She knew nothing more until she opened her eyes in response to light flickering across her eyelids. Shafts of yellow sunlight were slanting across the room through the opened slats of one of the louvred windows. She was still lying on the bed that had been a troubled haven during the night, the place where she had writhed in an agony of nausea and fever.

She blinked up at the ceiling and listened to the sound of waves falling on a unseen shore, the rustle of palm fronds in a breeze, the squawk of a parrot and the chuckling chatter of an animal that could be a monkey. All the sounds came through the two windows that faced each other so that air could waft through the room. Overhead a fan whirred softly. She glanced to the other side of the bed. César wasn't there, yet she was sure he had been there before she had fallen asleep.

Slowly Glenda pushed herself up into a sitting position, bracing herself against stabbing pains and the lurch of nausea. Both her head and stomach felt normal; no pains at all. The nightmare of sickness and fever was over. All that remained was an overwhelming feeling of embarrassment because she had been so ill here in César's hideaway and he had had to look after her.

Glancing at her watch, she noted that it was almost half past two. It must be the afternoon of the next day. Friday afternoon. She must get up and find César, interview him and then ask him to drive her back to the hotel.

Moving cautiously, she got off the bed and stood up. She felt a little weak, but she didn't sway and the floor didn't wobble or threaten to come up and hit her. She looked around the room. The walls were painted white and the floor

was covered with cool slate-coloured tiles with
mats woven from rushes scattered here and there.
The cushion covers on the bamboo chairs and
the bedcover were all made from heavy cream-
coloured cotton printed in bold designs of green,
red, and yellow. The same bright colours appeared
in a large painting, above the bed, of parrots and
leaves. Simple the room might be, but the furnish-
ings were of the best quality.

Her canvas shopping bag was on one of the
chairs. She took her beach robe from it and
slipped it on over the pyjama jacket, remembering
suddenly what César had said about her looking
sexy in the jacket. She frowned now at the way
he had treated her during the night. Sometimes
he had been kind and gentle, sometimes sharp
and authoritative, and sometimes irritably derisive. She had sensed he had regretted having
invited her to come here, and now she was
wishing she hadn't agreed to come. Her sickness
during the night might have destroyed their deli-
cate and tenuous relationship for ever. Today he
might feel he didn't want to be interviewed by
her because she had been such a nuisance to him.
In her experience, few men liked having to act as
nurse to a sick woman.

She left the bedroom and drifted into the
narrow passage, past the bathroom and through
an archway into a living-room. All one wall was
made of glass, sliding glass doors. The wall opposite had louvred wooden shutters, which
presumably could be folded back to allow air to
waft through the room from the open glass doors
and out through the openings now covered by

the shutters: a simple air-conditioning system. Through the wall of glass she could see a veranda and a view of Samana Bay, sparkling with reflected sunlight.

Two simple bamboo settees, with cushions covered in the same heavy cotton used in the bedroom, faced each other. Between them was a long low table. Near to a hatchway, through which she could see a kitchen, there was a small round dining-table and four chairs.

She was looking out at the view again when a voice spoke behind her.

'Mees Thompson?' it enquired.

She whirled round in surprise. A young man was standing by the doorway next to the hatchway. He was very thin and was dressed in cotton shorts and a blue T-shirt on which the favourite Dominican expression, 'No Problem', had been printed. His brown skin shone, his straight hair was ink-black and his large brown eyes were soft and gentle. When he smiled at her, parting his thick lips, he showed big white teeth.

'I'm Alberto Jones,' he said. 'I look after the house for the boss.'

'The boss? You mean Señor Estrada?' she asked. 'Where is he?'

'Right now I guess he is in La Pasquale. He'll be back later. He say for you to be at home here, ma'am. You feeling better now?'

'Much better, thank you.'

'Good, then I fix you something to eat.'

'You speak very good English, Alberto. Where did you learn it?' Glenda asked, her journalistic curiosity aroused.

'All my folks speak a sort of English, ma'am. My people come here from America long ago. They were slaves there. Here they were free. Now they are poor.' He grinned at her as if he had made a joke. 'So they would like to go back to America.'

'Do you speak Spanish, too?' she asked. She wished she could have interviewed him with her tape-recorder switched on to catch the inflections of his voice and his old-fashioned English.

'Yes, ma'am. We have to go to school in Spanish. We just speak English among ourselves or to any of the tourists. You like something to eat?'

'Yes, I would, please. Eggs? Poached eggs,' she suggested.

CHAPTER THREE

ALBERTO didn't know what Glenda meant by poached eggs, so she said she would show him how to cook them, and followed him into the kitchen. White cabinets gleamed in the sunlight against white walls. There were stainless steel sinks, a stainless steel gas cooker and shining worktops, and a view of the bay.

Finding Alberto an interested and quick learner, Glenda showed him how to poach eggs in a pan of boiling water. He found bread for her, butter and a bottle of pure water. She ate the meal in the living-room at the round table and questioned him about his family. He was nearly eighteen, he told her, and still going to school, although he was on holiday that week for the Easter Carnival. His father was a fisherman who lived in a house with his mother, brothers and sisters just along the shore from César's house.

'Papa catches mackerel, red snapper and king-fish in the bay. He casts nets from the small boat. It's dangerous work. Sometimes fishermen drown in storms in the bay. I don't want to do that work.' Alberto shook his head. 'I like to go to university to learn to be a lawyer or a school-teacher. Dr Estrada say he will help me do that if I work hard and pass exams. I like, too, to go to the States. My cousin Fernando, he lives there.

He plays baseball for a team in Kansas.'

'Really? Does he play for the Royals?'

'That's right,' Alberto nodded. 'Are you an American, ma'am?'

'No. I'm Canadian.'

'From Toronto?' Alberto's face sparkled with excitement and enthusiasm. 'You know the Blue Jays team?'

'Well, of course I know of them,' she replied, laughing at his excitement.

'Two friends of Fernando play for that team. It's a great team. Some day I go to Kansas and then to Toronto to see Fernando and his friends play.'

They talked for a little while longer about baseball and the World Series games of the previous year. Then Alberto produced her blouse and skirt. Both had been washed, dried and ironed by his mother, he told her. Glenda thanked him for them, asked him to thank his mother and, leaving him to clear away the dishes she had used, she went back to the bedroom.

It was great to feel normal again, she thought, as she showered in the bathroom, to feel that her head was its usual size and that she wasn't going to be sick again. In the bedroom she dressed in the clean clothes and folded the pyjama jacket, putting it on top of the chest of drawers. She was thinking of stripping the creased and tangled sheets from the bed when Alberto entered the room carrying clean sheets and pillow slips.

'I fix bed,' he said importantly. 'Boss say to tell you sit outside until he come, on the deck. It

is shady there now. You're not to sit in the sun,
he say.'

'All right, I'll do that,' said Glenda, thinking
again how autocratic César could be. Yet he
hadn't been like that in Montreal, as far as she
could remember.

She strolled back to the living-room. The house
wasn't very big. There seemed to be just one
bedroom, the living-room, the kitchen and bathroom. There was no special room where César
could do his writing. Where then did he write
when he was staying here? She swung around
away from the sliding glass doors. In a corner of
the room near the shuttered wall there was a
desk, above which were bookshelves. Hoping to
find something on the desk that would give her a
hint as to what César was working on for his
next book, she examined the few papers that lay
on the desk beside a small portable typewriter.
There was nothing among them that seemed
remotely related to a new novel. They were mostly
pamphlets printed in Spanish.

She looked up at the bookshelves. All the
books bore titles relating to medical matters.
There were books on anatomy, bio-chemistry and
tropical diseases. There were also magazines about
different aspects of medicine stuffed into the
shelves. All the books and magazines were in
English.

Dr Estrada, Alberto had told her, would help
him to get a university education if he worked
hard and passed exams. She assumed he had been
referring to César's father. These books, then,
must belong to him. But what were they doing

here in César's so-called hideaway? Did Dr
Estrada share the house with his son?

She lifted down one of the books and opened
it to look at the fly-leaf. A name was scrawled
on it: Rafael Estrada. Also written underneath
the name was an address in Chicago. She put the
book back and tried to remember anything that
César might have told her about his father. She
was sure he hadn't said anything about him being
a doctor of medicine. In fact, she was sure he
had told her that the senior Estrada was a high-
up government official. Of course, it was possible
he had been a doctor before he had become an
administrator.

Well, she would be able to find out when she
interviewed César. Meanwhile she would carry
out his orders, sit on the deck and relax, making
the most of being in such beautiful surroundings.
It was a perfect dream of a tropical paradise
come true, all modern comforts and conveniences
surrounded by whispering palms, set down by a
private beach on a secluded little bay protected
by rocky headlands.

From the shady veranda, steps led down to a
wide wooden deck on which deckchairs and loungers were set about a round table, and which, at
that time of the day, was shadowed by the house.
Stretching out on one of the loungers, Glenda
gazed out at the view.

When she had asked César the day before if
there would be anyone else staying at his house
in Samana, he had said yes, there would be, and
she had suggested his wife might be here and had
been rebuffed.

'We will not discuss my marriage,' he had said sharply. Why not? Why shouldn't he talk about his marriage? Was it possible that marriage had failed for him as it had for her? And if his wife wasn't here, who was the other person? The house was designed for only one person, and there were no signs of a woman living in it or having lived in it. Only a few clothes hung in the wardrobe in the bedroom. All were men's clothes, César's clothes.

The sound of a vehicle approaching the house and stopping, the slam of one of its doors, made her sit up and glance eagerly in the direction of the veranda. In a few minutes César appeared at the open doorway to the living-room. Glenda raised a hand and waved to him. He strode out and along the veranda, lithe and lean in another white shirt and dark blue jeans. He took the steps at one jump and came over to her.

Pleasure at seeing him flooded through her, surprising her. She swung her legs off the lounger and stood up, her hands reaching out to his, stretched out towards her. His slanted smile mocked her a little, but his eyes glowed with golden fire. His hands grasped hers strongly. Bending his head, he kissed her on both cheeks.

'It's good to find you here, up and about,' he murmured, still holding her hands. 'You're nice to come home to. I wish I could always find you waiting for me. How are you feeling now?'

'Much better,' she said. *Except for this strange racing of my pulses, this fire inside which you seemed to have ignited,* she said to herself. Aloud she added quickly, 'I'm so glad you've come at last. There's so much I have to ask you. But first I have to apologise for being such a nuisance yesterday and last night and to thank you for looking after me.'

'No problem.' He dropped her hands. 'I'm glad it wasn't anything more than it was, a touch of the sun or perhaps something you had eaten that had not been cooked properly. I was afraid at first you had picked up hepatitis. There's a lot of it about, for all the care we try to take, all the warnings we issue . . . ' He broke off, frowning, then shrugged. 'But no matter. You haven't got it. You are strong, healthy, well-fed and so can shake off disease easily. Not like some of the poor people I . . . ' Again he stopped, half-turning away from her. With a quick shake of his head he sloughed off his sombre mood and turned back to her, smiling, and a weakness, different from that she had suffered in the night, made her legs shake. 'Have you eaten?' he asked. 'Did Alberto prepare some food for you?'

'I showed him how to make poached eggs,' she replied. 'He didn't know how.'

'Good. Then you must be feeling well. Well enough to go swimming with me?'

'I'd like to,' she said, glancing at the beach and the smooth water, shimmering like gold silk in the light of the westering sun. 'But is there time? I'd like to interview you before you drive me back to the resort . . . '

'Later,' he interrupted autocratically.' Right now I must swim. I always do when I come back from . . . ' He broke off again with a muttered oath and turned away from her, making for the steps. 'Come on,' he ordered. 'Come and change. I know you have your swimsuit with you, I saw it in your canvas bag.'

Glenda didn't argue, but followed him into the house. After all, she wouldn't ever have this chance again to swim with him in the warm soft water. The day after tomorrow she would be gone, back to Canada, and she might never see him again. The thought didn't please her, so she pushed it away to the back of her mind. Sufficient unto the day, she thought with a smile at her own philosophical attitude. Let tomorrow and the next day take care of themselves. Today, or at least for the rest of today, she was going to make the most of being with César.

The water in the tiny cove was everything she had hoped it would be, buoyant and clear. They swam out to one of the headlands and went ashore to clamber over craggy rocks to a small plateau of grass on which was perched a steel framework supporting a navigation light. Beside the light more framework supported the blades of a modern windmill which revolved slowly in the light breeze. It was there presumably to provide power for the light.

'But of course, when there is no wind there is no light,' said César laughingly. 'That is typical of this country. Too bad if you're in a yacht approaching the harbour and this light goes out. Soon you are on those reefs over there and sinking fast.'

While they were swimming back to the beach the light changed as the sun set and by the time they were walking up to the house long purple shadows were slanting and the sea was tinted crimson and violet. Across the bay the distant hills were a dark silhouette against the fast spreading greyness. From the house, golden light spilled from windows and from the two lantern-shaped lamps attached to the walls under the veranda.

When she had changed from swimsuit into blouse and skirt again, Glenda took her tape-recorder, notebook and pen from her canvas bag and went back to the deck. César was already there in white shirt and shorts, his feet bare. He was standing by a barbecue watching charcoal heat up. Candlelight glimmered in a glass bowl on the round table. Two places had been set with table mats and silverware. As Glenda went down the steps, Alberto followed her with a wooden bowl full of salad and a basket of bread rolls.

'I'd like to start interviewing you now,' Glenda said determinedly to César. 'I know you're going to cook, but you could answer a few questions while you're watching the meat and I can make a note of your answers. Later on we can use the tape-recorder.'

'Tape-recorder?' Spinning on his bare heels, he turned to face her. By the light from the veranda lamps she could see he was frowning. 'You want to record what I say to you?' he asked.

'Yes. Most interviews are taped these days. It's so much better than having to decipher hurriedly scrawled notes and there's less chance of the article writer making a mistake.'

'But I don't want anything I say to be recorded,' he said coldly. He lifted steaks from a plate on a small table beside the barbecue and put them on the grid over the hot coals. Slowly they began to sizzle. 'I don't want anything I might tell you to be on tape for other persons to hear,' he added. He swung round again to give her a fiercely glinting, underbrowed glance. 'You will just have to be satisfied with your hurriedly scrawled notes,' he said drily. 'And make sure you don't make any mistakes.'

'Oh, really! You're making a lot of fuss about nothing,' Glenda said irritably. 'And no other person would hear any tape I might have of you talking. How could they?'

'You might mislay your tape-recorder as you mislaid your wallet. You yourself said you're often absentminded,' he jeered. 'Someone might find it, switch it on and hear whatever is on the tape.'

'But . . . ' She began to argue with him again, then changed her mind, realising that nothing would be gained by arguing with him. In fact, all might be lost. If she insisted on using the tape-recorder he might stubbornly refuse to answer any of her questions. 'Oh, all right,' she said, and sat down on one of the chairs placed at the table. Light from the veranda streamed very conveniently across the table. She opened her notebook, wrote his name on the first line of a fresh page and asked casually, 'You were born on this island, in the Republic, weren't you?'

'Don't you know that I was?' he answered aggravatingly. 'Didn't I tell you that in Montreal?' The scoffing note in his voice deepened. 'Ah, Glenda, you disappoint me. I was so sure you remembered everything I ever said to you all those years ago.' Spatula in hand, he appeared out of the shadows on the other side of the table, white shirt gleaming, white teeth glinting as he grinned at her. 'You were just the tiniest bit in love with me then, and a woman in love always remembers everything a lover says to her,' he added softly, tauntingly.

'We weren't lovers in Montreal,' she protested hotly.

'But you would have liked us to have been lovers and I would have liked to have been your lover,' he suggested wickedly.

His remark flicked her on the raw and, gritting her teeth, she sent a wary glance in his direction, but he had gone back to the barbecue and was watching the steaks.

'I can't think why you believe I would have liked us to be lovers,' she said stiffly. 'Have you forgotten Greg? I was engaged to him then. I wasn't in the least interested in having you for a lover.'

'Did you marry him?' he asked, not looking at her, but turning a steak over with the spatula.

'Yes.'

'So why don't you wear a wedding ring?' He shot the question at her sharply, spinning round on his heels again to look at her. Lean and agile, he moved fast but with control, muscles sliding easily under golden brown skin.

'Why don't you?' she countered with a lift of her chin.

'I never have.'

'I don't wear one because I divorced Greg four

years ago,' she said frankly, and watched from under drooping lashes for his reaction. In two strides César was beside her, and then, half sitting on the table, he looked down at her, his eyes alight with curiosity.

'How long were you married to him?'

'Oh, about two years.' Glenda lifted one shoulder in a careless shrug but couldn't look at him. He was too near to her, she decided, his warmth radiating out to her, the scents of his skin and hair tantalising her, making her want to reach out and touch his bare knee and slide her fingers upwards over his thigh.

'Why did you divorce him?' he asked softly.

'He didn't like me having a career. Or, at least, he didn't like my attempts to start a career. He didn't like me going away after stories. He thought I should stay at home all the time, look after the apartment, be there always when he came home from work . . . '

'Was that too much for him to ask?' he put in drily. 'Most men take a wife so that she'll be there at home waiting for them.'

'We should never have married. Or it would be better to say he shouldn't have married me. I . . . I couldn't do what he wanted. I shouldn't have let him marry me. I should have gone after what I wanted in a career first and married later. I knew I was to blame for the failure of our marriage just as much as he was. But . . . but I never expected him to cheat on me.' Her voice faltered and faded.

'He found someone else?' he deduced.

'Yes,' she admitted.

'And you were surprised?' He was scoffing at her again. 'You knew you weren't being the sort of wife he wanted, but you were surprised when he found a substitute? You were so naïve? My dear, it happens all the time.'

'I know that now. And I suppose I was naïve in thinking he wouldn't object to my pursuing a career, would accept my absences from home without cheating on me. After all, I had to accept his absences, and I didn't cheat.'

Glenda broke off abruptly, doodling on the page of her notebook. She was a little surprised at herself. This was the first time she had ever told anyone why she had been so disillusioned by her marriage to Greg, the sweetheart of her teenage and university years, who had become her husband almost as a matter of course, possibly because everyone—their families and friends —had expected them to marry.

'I'm glad you've told me,' murmured César, sliding to his feet.' This makes a big difference to my plans. Now you are here, we must make up for all the time we lost eight years ago, just because you were engaged to Greg.'

He moved away to the barbecue. Puzzled by his remarks, Glenda continued to doodle, frowning as she tried to remember the questions she wanted to ask him, realising irritably that he hadn't as yet answered her first question but had turned the tables on her and had adroitly interviewed her about her marriage to Greg. Sitting up straight, she pushed her hair behind her ears and called out to him,

'You haven't answered my question yet.'

'The steaks are done,' he replied coolly. 'I hope you can eat one of them.'

'Oh, yes, please. Swimming has made me very hungry. Can I do anything to help?'

'Could you?' he mocked, coming back to the table carrying two plates on which he had placed the steaks. 'From the description of your marriage to Greg I assume you're not what is termed domesticated.'

'Don't sneer at me,' she retorted. 'I can cook and prepare a meal as well as any other woman. I just don't see why a woman should be doing it all the time once she's married, why she should work like a slave for a man. Greg thought of me as a substitute for his mother.'

'Oh?' He set one of the plates before her and sat down opposite to her. 'You didn't sleep together, then?'

'Yes. What I mean is, he thought I should do all the things she'd always done for him and share his bed, too.' She took the salad bowl he was offering to her.

'He was only behaving like most men,' he drawled.

'Would you . . . I mean, do you expect your wife to wait on you all the time?'

'It doesn't matter to me what a woman does with her time as long as she makes me welcome when I go to bed with her,' he replied suggestively.

Across the table their eyes met and held. Glenda felt a strange little shiver go through her, even though the air was warm and there was no wind. Waves shushed on the beach. Somewhere somebody was playing a guitar. She looked down quickly, unable to face the message in César's eyes any longer, and picked up her fork. Somehow she had to change the subject. The approach of Alberto with a carafe of wine and two glasses eased the tension.

After Alberto had gone, César said casually, 'You like Alberto? Find him interesting?'

'We discussed baseball,' she said, relaxing.' And he told me that your father is going to help him go to university.'

'My father?' He seemed puzzled.

'Dr Estrada, he said. And I just assumed he meant your father. And I did notice there are a lot of medical books on the shelves in the living-room.'

He made no comment because he was busy eating, and then he drank some wine. Setting down his empty glass, he reached for the carafe and poured more wine for himself.

'I thought I told you about my family when I was in Montreal,' he said.

'All you told me was that your father is in the Dominican government. You didn't tell me he's a doctor of medicine,' she replied.

'He isn't. My mother is the doctor; my father is a lawyer by profession,' he replied, then snapped at her, 'What are you doing?'

She was fitting the wire of the small microphone belonging to the tape-recorder into the box, and plugging it in. She set the microphone in the middle of the table pointing in his direction so that it would pick up his voice when he answered her questions.

'I can't take notes while I'm eating,' she explained calmly. 'And what you're telling me about your family is important to the article I'm going to write. I want to know all about your family background.' She switched on the tape-recorder. 'Now, what was it you said about your father, that he's in the government? What position does he hold?'

'No!' César spat the word out and, stretching out an arm, picked up the small microphone, tugged the wire out of the socket on the tape-recorder and flung the microphone away, over the wooden rail of the deck into the darkness of the clustering shrubs.

'What do you think you're doing?' exclaimed Glenda, springing to her feet.

'This.' He had stepped around the table. He swept the tape-recorder to the floor of the deck where it landed with a thump. Close to her again, he returned her glare of outrage with a glittering glare of his own. 'I have told you that I do not want anything I say to be taped. You will make notes or remember in your head anything I say to you, anything I tell you,' he grated through set teeth. 'Do you understand?'

'No, I don't. I didn't think you'd be like this, so unco-operative or so violent, and I can only hope you haven't broken my recorder. If you have you can buy me a new one!'

She knelt on one knee to pick up the recorder, but he moved faster than she did and when her hands reached out to the black box they were taken by his. He was kneeling, as she was, on the same side of the box. The grasp of his hands was warm and the glitter had gone from his eyes. He was looking at her with a dark, wary expression in his eyes.

'I hope I haven't broken the recorder, too,' he said softly. 'But if I have I will buy you a new one as you ask, just as long as you don't use it when you're interviewing me. I had to show you somehow how much I dislike having what I say recorded, how much it offends me.' He looked down at their clasped hands. 'I don't like being interviewed either, and I wish you wouldn't interview me. If you knew what it has been like these past few months for . . . ' he hesitated fractionally, almost as if drawing back from something he had been about to say, then said quickly, 'for me.'

'What do you mean? What are you talking about?' she asked. Being close to him in oddly intimate circumstances was clouding her normally cool objectivity. When he spoke to her softly and looked at her warmly she felt she wanted to give in and do anything he wanted, to give him everything he asked for, even herself. Afraid of the sudden rush of submissiveness to his will, she pulled her hands from his, picked up the recorder and stood up, placing it on the table again. 'What has been happening to you during the past few months?' she asked again, turning to him as he stood up.

'I wish I could tell you,' he said mysteriously, going back to his chair and sitting down. 'But I can't,' he added, and picked up his wine glass. 'Please sit down and finish your meal.'

Glenda sat down, still baffled by his behaviour,

wondering how she could best overcome his
objection to being interviewed.

'I don't understand why you invited me to
come here if you feel so strongly about being
interviewed,' she said. 'You could have refused
yesterday.'

'I know I could. But you forget you're an old
friend, Glenda; it was hard for me to refuse you.
Besides, I wanted you to come here and stay with
me for a while,' he replied quietly. 'To return
your hospitality of eight years ago.'

She finished eating, laid down her knife and
fork, and looked across the table at him.

'I suppose you feel your privacy is invaded
when you're interviewed,' she said musingly. 'I
know that some journalists don't care what questions they ask and often distort the truth. It's a
price that celebrities have to pay, and you're a
celebrity now, whether you like it or not. People
want to know all about you; they want to know
what made you write that novel. It's just natural
curiosity. It isn't meant unkindly. I wish you'd
change your mind and let me interview you, for
old times' sake. I can't use the tape-recorder now
because I can't find the microphone in the dark,
but please will you answer my questions about
your background and about the novel? Please,
César?'

She leaned towards him, her face illuminated
by the candlelight. He leaned forward too, smiling
a little, his eyes dancing with mockery.

'Careful, pretty moth,' he murmured. 'You
might get singed.'

'César, please be serious!'

'I am serious. You are pretty with your pink and white skin, your shining grey eyes. I have always thought so and I would very much prefer to make love to you than to answer your questions.' He reached across the table to touch her hand. No longer mocking, his eyes seemed to smoulder with golden fire. 'And we could make love, you and I, here, tonight. We could experience romance together, make real the dream we dreamt eight years ago.'

Glenda's lips parted as she drew a shaky breath and her heart seemed to swell, become too big to be contained in its cage. Her hand turned under his, the palm opening to receive his fingers and closing about them. She looked right into his candlelit eyes and her head reeled as if she had drunk too much wine. Never before in the whole of her life had she felt desire pulse so strongly through her as it did at that moment. More than anything, she wanted to do as he suggested, to make love with him and make their dream of romance come true.

Then, like a splash of iced water, the memory that he was married hit her. She stiffened, slid her hand from under his and shook her head.

'I wish you'd be serious,' she whispered.

'I am serious,' he said again. 'You'll see.' He pushed back his chair. 'But right now the time has come for dessert. We'll eat fruit salad made by Alberto's mother, who was grateful for your bag of fruit, and drink rich Dominican coffee and perhaps a liqueur.'

He scooped up their empty plates from the table and was gone with a leap up the steps to the veranda. Glenda heard him calling to Alberto.

CHAPTER FOUR

MORE disturbed than she cared to admit by his assault on her emotions, Glenda sank back in her chair. She couldn't believe that what was happening to her was real. It must be an illusion, a fantasy bred of the atmosphere, of the soft dark tropical night, the lilting guitar music, the fretted shadows of palm leaves, the murmur of waves against the shore and among the rocks, the shimmer of moonlight on the sea.

A woman like her, disillusioned by a youthful and unsuccessful marriage with a young man she had known most of her life, knew better than this, she argued with herself; knew better than to fall for the subtle seduction as practised by an experienced, sophisticated man like César. She couldn't possibly have fallen in love with him again within only a few hours of having met him for the first time in eight years.

Yet how else could she explain this excitement that was boiling in her veins in response to his suggestion that they picked up their friendship where they had left off and take it further, indulge in the pleasures of passion with each other? It wasn't the first time since her marriage to Greg had been dissolved that she had been approached by a man with the idea that she should go to bed with him, but not having felt any desire to make love with any of them, she had found it easy to turn them down.

Tonight she felt differently. Tonight, if César invited her to sleep with him, she knew deep down inside her that she would have difficulty in refusing him. Physically he attracted her as no other man ever had, not even Greg. She longed to touch him, caress him, be close to him, and the urge wasn't new to her. She had felt it at their last meeting and had shied away from it because she had promised to marry Greg. Now she had the opportunity to satisfy the demands of her desire to be closer to him. Tonight, as he had said, they could make come true the dream of romance they had apparently shared, without knowing it, eight years ago.

But she mustn't do it this time, because he was married. How could she do to his wife what Antoinette Lavallée had done to her? How could she help him cheat on his wife? Never, never could she take a man away from his wife as Antoinette had taken Greg away from her. Never. Her dream of romance would have to remain a dream after all.

Sighing, she turned to her notebook and began to write down the few bits of information he had given her. Born in the Dominican Republic. Father a lawyer, working for the government? Mother a doctor of medicine. Her pen hovered above the paper as she considered that piece of information and she frowned, thinking of the medical books in the living-room, the name on the fly-leaf of one of them. Rafael was definitely not a woman's name.

César came back carrying a tray, and set it down on the table. The aroma of freshly brewed coffee rose from the coffee-pot on the tray. He set a dish of fruit salad before her and began to pour coffee into the two cups.

'What year were you born?' she asked, determined to hide her feelings about him behind a cool professional façade. She was there because she wanted to interview him and for nothing else, and as soon as she had enough information she would leave, no matter how much it hurt to leave him.

'But Glenda,' he said mockingly, 'you must know my age. We were close friends in Montreal. Surely I told you my age then?'

Why did he keep parrying her questions? she wondered. Perhaps he really meant what he had said, that he didn't like being interviewed. Or . . . the suspicion shot up like a fast-growing fungus in her mind . . . perhaps he had something to hide from her, something that might change her feelings about him.

'All right,' she said coolly. 'If you won't tell me, I'll just have to guess. You're thirty-six. Right?'

'If you say so.' Across the table his glance mocked her. Firmly she tightened her lips, refusing to be baited.

'And your father is in the government?'

'Not any more. He is retired.' He answered with a shrug as if he considered that piece of information unimportant.

'And what about your mother? Is she still alive? And did she train to be a doctor in this country?'

'Yes, she still lives. With my father, too. Theirs has been a long and happy marriage. She didn't train in this country. She is an American by birth, from Milwaukee in Wisconsin. She came here with a group of young doctors to work on a voluntary basis in a new hospital that was founded years ago with American financial aid. She met my father and they married.' César gave her another derisive glance. 'Am I being serious enough for you, Glenda?' he asked tauntingly, and raised a hand to his hair. 'I'll just add a detail for your more romantic readers. My mother is just as responsible for the colour of my hair as that English pirate I once told you about. She is tall and fair, Scandinavian in appearance. Her ancestors emigrated from Sweden to America in the last century. I will even tell you her name: she is Ingrid Jensen. So you see, I am a mixture of north and south, light and dark, my belief in free thought and free love, inherited from my Scandinavian forebears, always at war with the passionate possessiveness inherited from my Spanish forebears. It is a difficult temperament to live with. But that is enough for now. Stop scribbling, eat your fruit cocktail and drink your coffee. There is Tia Maria, too.'

Glenda did as he ordered, put down her pen and picked up her dessertspoon. The fruit cocktail was chunky with pineapple, tangy with orange and smooth with sliced bananas. The coffee was rich and hot, the Tia Maria sweet, yet with a kick. She was silent while she ate and drank, thinking over what he had told her about his mother and also those hints about his own temperament. That hadn't come through in his book, she thought. He had revealed nothing of himself in the novel at all, had seemed concerned only to give an objective portrayal of the more usual types of Latin-Americans. She picked up her pen again.

'You didn't tell me about your mother when you lived in Montreal,' she said. 'Do you have any brothers or sisters?'

'One brother,' he replied tersely.

'Did you live in Santa Domingo as a child? Did you go to school there?' she asked.

'Perhaps tomorrow,' he replied.

'Pardon me?' She glanced at him, puzzled by his answer. He was leaning back in his chair. Smoke rose from the cigar he had lit and which he was holding in his right hand.

'Perhaps I'll tell you more tomorrow,' he said. 'I don't feel like answering any more of your questions right now.' He laughed softly. 'To tell the truth, I am finding answering them more and more taxing on my imagination. Making up stories is not really my forte.'

'But you're a novelist,' she argued. 'Making up stories, or rather fictionalising facts, is your profession. Please don't stop; please answer the rest of my questions now. I . . . I can't stay until tomorrow. I must go back to the hotel tonight.'

'I'll answer the rest of your questions tomorrow. Only if you stay the night here with me will I tell you more about myself. That is the price you have to pay if you want to inteview me.' César leaned towards her and added softly, 'You'll stay,

Glenda, and we'll make real the dream we once dreamt but couldn't make come true because you were engaged to Gregory and were too young, too highly principled to practise free love.'

Once again excitement boiled through her in response to his suggestive invitation. The smouldering warmth of his gaze, the slight upward tilt of the corner of his mouth, both importuned her, tempting her to agree to stay the night with him and perhaps reach with him the dizzy heights of ecstasy, if there was such an exalted state. Her puritan upbringing, her liberated education and her emotionless experience with Greg had all led her to believe that ecstasy was a romantic myth created by men to seduce women.

'I can't stay. I can't stay and do what you want to do,' she said, fighting her desire to love and possess him with all the powers of reason at her command. 'And I'm not willing to pay the price you ask for an interview. I'll make do with the information I have already and my own knowledge of your book.' She pushed back her chair and stood up. 'I left a note for my friend Ida in the cabin we're sharing at the hotel. I told her that if I wasn't back last evening I would be back some time today. If I don't go back, if I'm not there before midnight, she'll worry and start looking for me. Please drive me back to the hotel now, César. That is, if you value our friendship.'

He stood up, too, and squashed out the cigar in an ashtray. Slowly he came round the table to her. Tall and straight, he stood before her, his eyes gleaming like amber in his shadowed face.

'I don't value our friendship enough to drive

you back to the hotel,' he said quietly and force-fully. 'You will stay the night here. I have no wish to be just your friend; I want to be your lover, too. I wanted to be your lover when we last met, but there was no time, no opportunity. Now we have both. I'm not going to let you go back to the hotel or to Canada without us first consummating our love for each other.'

'But . . . but Ida . . . ' she muttered.

'Forget about Ida,' he said, taking hold of her arms, sliding his hands upwards, his palms warm on her skin. 'She won't worry about you. This morning while you were sleeping and recovering I drove to the hotel and informed the manage-ment you wouldn't be back there until Sunday morning, just before you have to go to the airport to catch the flight to Toronto. I was allowed to go to your cabin and fortunately Ida was there. She packed your case for me when I told her you hadn't been well, and she sent a message to you saying you aren't to worry about her but to make the most of your stay here with me.'

He began to draw her towards him and, abso-lutely amazed by what he had just told her, she let him. 'And that's what we're going to do,' he continued. 'We're going to make the most of being together tonight, tomorrow and tomorrow night. We're going to have that love affair we never had, a delayed but much-hoped-for affair. You won't deny that you dreamt of being with me, of making love with me eight years ago?'

'No, I don't deny it,' she whispered.

'Then let us make up for lost time.' His breath feathered her lips enticingly. 'Kiss me, Glenda,' he whispered. 'You know you want to. Kiss me to show me you forgive me for planning to make you stay with me tonight. Kiss me to show me you want to stay as much as I want you to stay.'

He didn't plead. He ordered, softly and gently, it was true, but also demandingly, and her lips parted in instinctive response, even though they had not yet felt the titillation of his tongue. Her hands went up to frame his face and to draw his lips down to hers.

As soon as she felt the warm hardness of his lips against hers, a door inside her that had been closed a long time burst open and all her pent-up passion gushed forth. Giving in to that rush of heat, she slid her fingers up his lean cheeks into the wiry thickness of his hair. Her tongue flickered wantonly against his lips. As if licked by flame, he gasped, his mouth opening over hers. His arms slid around her and she was crushed against his lean length until she could feel the hard thrust of his maleness through her thin skirt.

For a few moment she was lost in a whirl of sexual desire, conscious only of exquisite sensations tingling along her skin and needling through her flesh. The burning heat of his skin struck through the thinness of his shirt, radiating through her blouse until she felt on fire. Smokily sweet was the taste of his mouth to her tongue, inducing it to linger there in a tenderly tantalising duel. She pressed closer to him without knowing it, her fingers clinging to his curls, her hardened breasts pushing against his chest.

Then, slowly, insidiously, there crept into the

throbbing darkness of her mind a cold thought. César was married. He belonged to another woman just as once Gregory had belonged to her, or so she had naïvely believed, until she had found out about Antoinette Lavallée.

All passion froze within her. She slid her lips from beneath his and opened her eyes. She withdrew her hands from his hair and stepped back from him. His arms fell to his sides. Straight and still he stood, his lamplit sand-coloured hair making an aureole for his dark face, his white shirt gleaming, his eyebrows slanting in a frown.

'What is wrong?' he demanded.

'Nothing,' lied Glenda, turning away from him towards the table.

'Don't lie!' he rapped. 'And don't believe I'm so insensitive that I didn't notice you go cold suddenly, freeze up like your northern lakes do in the winter. You didn't like the way I kissed you back, perhaps,' he added jeeringly. 'Didn't you expect me to respond to your blatant invitation to make love to you? Are you the sort of woman who kisses and regrets, kisses and then runs away, afraid of commitment, afraid of going all the way?'

'No. No, it wasn't that. I . . . I just remembered something,' she muttered wildly, alarmed by his accurate guess. She was afraid of commitment, of going all the way with him. She was afraid of being hurt.

'What?' He seized her arm roughly and pulled her round to face him. Crackling with light now that he was no longer in the shadows, his eyes seemed to stab into hers. 'Tell me what you remembered?'

She drew a deep breath and swallowed hard. She would have to tell him the truth. She couldn't lie to him when he looked at her like that.

'I remembered that you're married,' she said frankly.

'And that matters to you?' A sort of scornful surprise lilted in his voice and his long lips curled sardonically as if he didn't believe her statement.

'Yes, it does matter. Very much.'

His grasp on her arm lightened and his fingers began to move seductively over her skin again, sending tiny erotic messages dancing along her nerves and causing her to shiver pleasurably and involuntarily.

'Please, don't do that,' she whispered, and pulled her arm away from his fingers. 'I don't want you to touch me. And I have to tell you I can't make love with another woman's husband or another woman's lover. It . . . it's the way I'm made.'

'Not even when you're in love with that husband or that lover?' he challenged her.

'Not even then,' she asserted, her head held high. 'And I'm not in love with you.'

'I think you are,' he retorted, and his smile threatened to destroy for ever the cool command she was managing to assert over her feelings. Leaning towards her, he twisted one finger in a strand of her hair. 'And I'm in love with you, sweet, serious puritan.'

'Oh, no! You mustn't be,' she cried. 'Think of your wife, please. If I could have guessed this would happen I wouldn't have agreed to come here with you. You said there would be someone else here. I didn't think we would be alone.'

'There is someone else here, at least part of the time. Alberto is here.' Laughter rippled in his voice. 'Not that he can be considered as a chaperon!'

'You must see I can't stay with you, and I'm not going to stay. Let me go!'

A quick swipe to his wrist with the side of her hand made him withdraw his hand from her hair. Turning, Glenda fled up the steps to the veranda, not really sure of where she was going, knowing only instinctively that she had to get away from his powerful attraction before she lost all control and gave in to his seductive tactics.

Through the open doorway into the living-room she rushed and, turning right, darted along the passage to the bedroom. The darkness of the room was dappled with light from one of the veranda lamps. She went in quickly, walked into something on the floor hidden in the shadow, jarred her shins and, losing her balance, went headlong over whatever it was to sprawl on the floor.

She was struggling to sit up when light dispersed the shadows. César stood in the doorway, his hand just dropping away from the light switch on the wall.

'What did you do?' he exclaimed, and strode over to her. He dropped to one knee close to her. She looked past him at the dark shape of her suitcase, now lying flat on the floor after she had collided with it.

'I fell over that!' she seethed. 'Why did you have to leave it in the middle of the floor?'

'I didn't. I gave it to Alberto to bring in here. You must excuse him, he is not very well house-trained. He is willing to learn, like the rest of our people, but it will take time to teach them how to behave as porters or bellboys. Are you hurt?'

'I banged my shins.'

'Let me see.' His hand went out to lift her skirt away from her legs.

'No!' she shouted at him, and jumped to her feet. César stood up, too, and grinned mockingly at her.

'So you don't like me to touch you. I wonder why?' he scoffed softly. 'But why did you come in here?'

'To collect my things. I'm not leaving without my belongings.'

'You'd really leave without finishing the interview?' he queried, raising his eyebrows. 'Why?'

'I've told you why. I can't pay the price. I can't stay the night with you, knowing you're married.'

'And how do you propose to get back to the hotel tonight?' he asked, stepping towards her stealthily, his eyes dancing with devilry.

'I . . . I'll walk to the town,' she said wildly, backing away from him. 'Unless you'll be reasonable and drive me to the hotel on the headlands. I can stay the night there.'

'But I don't feel very reasonable,' he purred, still advancing on her. 'I feel passionate, on fire with desire for you . . . '

'Oh, don't be silly,' she faltered. 'You can't be. That doesn't happen to . . . to real people.'

'But I can assure you it does,' he retorted. 'Let me give you a taste of how I feel.'

He moved swiftly, his arms reaching out and grabbing her. His lips swooped arrogantly to hers. Hungrily and bruisingly he kissed hers, and amazingly she didn't resent the domineering possessiveness of his mouth as his tongue explored the smoothness of her lips before thrusting into the hollow of her mouth.

She was actually enjoying the way he was kissing her, as if he wanted her more than any other woman he had ever known. His hands slid tantalisingly down her spine to the small of her back and then his fingers dug into her buttocks as he pressed her hips against his, so that she felt his arousal and, feeling it, became aroused herself, returning the kiss willingly, succumbing to its head-spinning flavour.

Dark and dangerous was the tide of passion that swept through her, threatening to swamp all her hard-held principles concerning making love with men who were married to other women. She made one last effort to stem that tide, wrenching her mouth from his, but she was too shaky to step away from him this time. She leaned helplessly against his chest, dizzy with desire, drawing in deep panting breaths. Under her ear she could hear the excited thud of his heart, then felt the tormentingly tender touch of his fingertips at her throat, under her chin, along the line of her jaw.

'We mustn't do this,' she gasped. Yet even as she spoke her own lips betrayed her. Finding themselves close to the hollow at the base of his throat, they turned into it and rubbed against the pulsing warm skin lovingly.

'Why not, if we like doing it and want to do it?' César asked softly, winding a hand in the hair at the back of her head and pulling her head up and back so that he could look into her eyes. In the soft golden light shed by the two bamboo-shaded lamps of the room his eyes seemed to glow.

'Your marriage,' Glenda said frantically, trying to push away from him and finding herself trapped by his arms. 'Please, think of your wife and how she'd feel it she knew I was here and what you want to do with me.'

'I don't believe it.' His lips curved into a mocking smile while his fingers, drifting round from the back of her head, tantalised her throat again. 'I don't believe you really care how she would feel if she knew I've just kissed you to show you I want you. You know you want me, so why should you care about her?'

'Because I know what it's like to be in her position. I know what it's like to find my husband has been sleeping with another woman while I've been away. I divorced Greg because I found out he'd been cheating on me with Antoinette, and I just can't do that to your wife. I don't want to be like Antoinette!'

A frown of impatience darkened his face. His arms dropped to his sides. He opened his mouth as if to say something, changed his mind and closed it. With a shake of his head he turned away from her and walked over to the door. Shaky with confused emotions, relief battling with a deep ache of disappointment, Glenda swayed slightly without his support and sat down quickly on the bed behind her. She felt thoroughly wretched as she suppressed a longing to go after him, fling her arms around him and invite him to kiss her again so that she could show him she still wanted him, even though her own moral code dictated that she couldn't have him.

In the doorway he paused and spun round to look back at her, and again she had the impression he was going to say something to her. But he didn't; he just stood and looked at her. The space between them vibrated with a tension that made her want to scream. Then, slowly, he came back and sat down beside her on the bed. Lifting one of her hands from her lap, he raised it to his lips and held it there for a few seconds, all the time looking into her eyes, his own eyes dark and sober.

'If I told you that my marriage means as little to me as yours to Greg now means to you, and that you wouldn't be making love with another woman's husband if you make love with me tonight, would you do it?' he asked.

'Is it over then, your marriage?' she queried hopefully, studying his face, trying to fathom what facts lay behind his question.

'It never really began.' One corner of his mouth quirked in wry amusement and dark lashes veiled his eyes suddenly as he looked down at their entwined hands which seemed to be behaving independently of either of them, fingers stroking skin and occasionally squeezing suggestively.

'You mean . . . ' She broke off in puzzlement,

then added quickly, 'I'm sorry it didn't work out for you.'

'You don't have to be sorry. I have no regrets.' Again there was a slight suspicion of laughter in his voice. 'But I thought I should say something to you about it. Does it make a difference to how you feel about staying with me and making love with me?'

His eyelids lifted slowly, heavily, and he looked right at her again, his eyes lambent with golden fire. Heat flooded through her. She seemed to be possessed by another fever, a different fever. Her whole body throbbed and ached with the sexual need his kisses had aroused in her. She licked her recently bruised lips and his glance slanted to them. His own lips parted as if in invitation.

'It makes a big difference,' she whispered.

Blind to everything except the sensual curve of his lips, deaf to everything except the beat of her own heart, her mind spinning with the inhaled scents of his skin and hair, she swayed involuntarily towards him and put a hand on his thigh to save herself from falling against him. Under the skin left bare by his shorts, hard sinews flexed in response to her touch.

'There is no successor to Greg?' he asked, seeming determined to extend the tension between them. 'You have no lover back in Canada?'

'I have no lover,' she said, and gave in to the urge to touch him again. Raising a hand, she traced the shape of his lips, then the line of his jaw. Her fingers slid down his throat and within the slit of his shirt. She heard the sharp hiss of his indrawn breath.

'You should have. You're too pretty to live
alone. You should have a lover. I used to think
so years ago, and I would have made love to you
if you had looked at me just once as you're
looking at me now, touched me as you're touching
me now,' he murmured, and bent to kiss the
vulnerable curve between her neck and shoulder.
Suggestive tingles tripped along her nerves and
she gasped with delight when he nibbled at her
earlobe, then blew gently into the orifice.

'Oh, I wish I'd known you felt like that about
me. I wished I'd known,' she groaned. She was
really in the grip of the fever now and not caring
at all about what she did, her arms going around
him, her hands caressing his nape, tangling in his
hair as more sizzling sensations seared her when
his fingers drifted across the uplifted hardened
points of her breasts beneath the silk of her
blouse.

'So, will you let me love you now?' César
rubbed his slightly bristly cheek against hers, a
subtle, enticingly different caress that undermined
her completely.

'Yes. Oh, yes!'

Her answer floated like a feather against his
hovering lips. She had a brief glimpse of his face
darkening with desire and then he was kissing
her again and pushing her back against the pillows
at the head of the bed.

'Señor!' Alberto's voice spoke loudly. 'Come
quick, I need you!'

César groaned deep in his throat, lifted his
head and twisted to his feet. Opening her eyes,
Glenda saw him stride to the doorway. She

couldn't see Alberto and assumed he was in the passageway. She heard César snapping questions in Spanish and then he had gone from her view and she was alone.

CHAPTER FIVE

DISAPPOINTMENT quickly cooled the fever of desire. Sitting up, Glenda swung off the bed, smoothed her hair back with her hands and wandered towards the doorway. She was halfway along the passageway when she met César coming back. His face was set in grim lines.

'Oh! What is it? What's happened?' she exclaimed.

'Nothing that you need be concerned about,' he said coolly, but he seized both her hands in his. 'I have to go out for a while, but I will be back. You will stay, Glenda, please. You won't run away from me again?'

'No, I won't run away,' she said. 'I'll be here when you come back.'

'Gracias,' he said fervently, and kissed both her hands this time before turning on his heel and leaving her. When she reached the living-room she heard the truck's engine roar into life. There was no sign of Alberto and she assumed the boy had gone with César.

The house seemed very empty without César's dynamic presence, she thought, so she wandered outside and went down to the deck. The warm air enfolded her like a lover's arms, and caressed her skin, yet for all its warmth she shivered. Alberto had cleared everything away from the table and pushed it to one side. Glenda sat down on one of the loungers and lay against the raised back of it. Higher in the sky now, the moon shone down, its silver radiance illuminating everything with a cold brilliance. From a distance, across the water, came the sound of dance music.

Where had César gone, and why? Something of importance must have occurred for him to wrench himself away from her just when she had given in to him and had agreed to make love with him. Something to do with his family? Or with his wife?

Her breath caught in her throat. Oh, God, perhaps he had been lying to her when he had said he was no longer married. No, he hadn't really said that. He had just said that if she made love with him she wouldn't be making love with another woman's husband, and that this marriage had never really begun, and she had assumed that the marriage had never been consummated so had probably been annulled.

There had been that lilt of laughter in his voice, as if he had been amused by what he had been saying to her. Yes, he could have been lying to her. And she had been so ready to believe him that she hadn't questioned him closely, hadn't asked him outright if he was divorced. She was so in love with him, she was willing to believe anything he told her about himself. She wanted him to be unmarried so that she would have no qualms about making love with him.

Sitting up, she hunched her knees, wrapped her arms around them and rested her chin on them. Although the fever of desire she had experienced in the bedroom had cooled, Glenda's pulses still throbbed and low down inside her there was a raw ache.

How she wished Alberto hadn't come when he had! How she longed for César to come back, take her in his arms and kiss her into submission. Never in the whole of her life had she felt like this. Neither Greg nor any other man had been able to arouse her in this way. If there had been any other man able to excite her to the point where she was willing to cast caution to the winds and indulge in sexual pleasure for its own sake, she wouldn't have been there, on that deck, waiting and listening for César's return.

She sat for a long time, thinking about him. He was something of an enigma and not always like the man she had known in Montreal. There had been times in Montreal when she had thought him to be shy. Many of her memories of being with him eight years ago were very blurred, she discovered. So often they had been with other people when they had met in parties, at dances. Only on two occasions could she remember having been alone with him, and those memories were the most vivid, the ones she had treasured over the years without admitting to herself that she had. On those occasions he had been most like he was here: lively, a little sardonic, often teasing her and not at all shy or dreamy. Looking back now, it seemed to her that she had known two Césars.

Ridiculous. She shook her head, laughing at her own flight of fantasy. How could there be two men with sand-coloured hair and olive skin?

Only if they were twins.

Again she laughed, shaking her head. If there

were twin Estrada brothers, she would know,
wouldn't she? They would have different first
names; they wouldn't both be called César.

Unless one had pretended to be the other.

A cold chill seeped through her at the thought.
She tried to shake it away again; conjecturing
like this was silly. Why would one of them, if
there were twin Estrada brothers, pretend to be
the other? For what reason would either of them
want to deceive her? She didn't want to know,
she decided. She was letting her imagination run
away with her. And hadn't César himself admitted
this evening that he had a sort of split personality
because his father was of Spanish descent and his
mother was Scandinavian? That could account
for the differences in his behaviour when she had
known him in Montreal, couldn't it? Of course it
could.

Should she tell him of her suspicions? She tried
to imagine herself asking him outright who he
was, when he came back, and failed. She couldn't
ask him because she didn't want to know that
she might have been deceived, she realised. She
wanted to believe there was only one man like
him, the man she could have fallen in love with
eight years ago if she had been free, and had
probably fallen in love with now; the man who
said he was in love with her and wanted their
once-dreamed-of romance to come true.

It was past eleven o'clock when César returned
at last, and Glenda was lying on the bed in the
hot darkness, under the purring ceiling fan, trying
to woo sleep. He came into the room like the
wind she had been longing for, striding over to
the bed and sitting down on it beside her, a

darker shape in the light dappled gloom.

'You aren't ill again?' he asked sharply.

'No. I was trying to sleep, but it's so hot. Even with the fan going it's too hot.'

'So why wear this?' He flicked fingers against her short cotton nightgown. 'It's best to sleep in the nude on a night like this.' He sprang up from the bed and with a few swift movements stripped off his shirt. Tossing it aside, he dropped his shorts to the floor, revealing that he was wearing brief underpants. Turning to her, he held out a hand to her. She put hers in it and he pulled her from the bed into his arms. His hungry kiss blistered her lips and through the thin cotton of her nightgown his hands burned.

'I'm sorry I had to leave you,' he whispered, rubbing her cheek with his. 'Do you still want me?'

'I want you,' she replied shyly. Under her hands his skin was hot, moist with sweat, and the male smell of him was like an inhaled drug to her brain, making her dizzy.

'And I want you,' he murmured deeply, and once again his mouth dominated hers.

But not for long. When the kiss was over he took her hand again and pulled her after him as he strode from the room along the passage and into the bathroom. There he coaxed her with more caresses and tender laughter out of her nightgown and into the shower with him. Under tepid sluicing water he soaped her with flower-scented soap, mocking her shyness at such intimacy, his fingers lingering tantalisingly in vulnerable hollows or dancing tormenting tattoos on her breasts.

'And now you do it for me,' he ordered softly, handing Glenda the soap. 'In this game of sensual love you must learn to give as well as take, *querida*. You must learn to touch and stroke, give me pleasure as well as receive it from me. You know, for all you've been married, there is a freshness and a softness about you that excites me so much I could take you here and now. But I want more than that. I want you to take me as I take you. Now show me what you can do.'

He turned his back to her. Her body tingling all over from his caresses as well as stimulated by the gentle sting of the showering water, her mind reeling under the onslaught of his nearness and the sight of his broad glistening back, lean hips and taut buttocks, she began to rub the soap over his skin, vaguely amazed at herself for being in such an intimate situation.

'Use your imagination, *querida*,' murmured César, turning his head and speaking to her over one shoulder. 'Make for both of us an experience we'll always remember and treasure.'

As her hands moved rhythmically over his back she felt a sharp reaction low down in her own body. The movement of her arm and hand caused her to sway slightly and had a strange dazing effect on her mind. She didn't notice when the soap slipped from her hand but continued to touch him, her palms slipping easily over his skin. Slowly he turned to face her.

'Go on,' he murmured thickly.

From that moment she was swept on by the pounding torrent of her own desire. Her hands roved urgently over his elegant suntanned body. Encouraged by his murmured endearments as well as by the touch of his hands sliding over her skin, she lost all her shyness and began to kiss him, pressing her lips anywhere, exulting in his gasps of pleasure. Excited beyond all coherent thought, she responded with wild abandon when he held her, slippery as a mermaid between his hands, and kissed her. There was no thought of right or wrong, only a strong wish to pleasure him as he was pleasuring her, yet when the kiss was over she lay against him, as they still stood under the shower, tears springing to her eyes at the idea that such intimacy wouldn't last forever. The delight they were sharing would pass all too quickly. On Sunday she would leave and fly to Canada and César would stay here.

As if sensing her distress, he was gentle with her, patting her dry with a big towel and persuading her to do the same for him. They sprinkled each other laughingly with talc, then returned to the bedroom to wrap themselves in their robes, she in her beach robe, he in a short silk kimono. Glenda could have asked him then about his brother, whether they resembled each other in any way, but she drew back, not wanting to spoil the moments of intimacy, afraid she might find out something she wouldn't like and would be unable to go all the way with him to satisfy the urgings of passion.

Out on the veranda he led her, to a wide double hammock woven from thick cord and scattered with soft cushions. The moon, a silver disc, shone out of a sky made from blue-black velvet. From the distance came the sound of drums and guitars—the band in the hotel's disco, César told her—carrying across the placid bay.

'Do you remember the disco on Rue St Paul in old Montreal where we all used to go to dance?' she asked him as they lay side by side in the swaying, dangerously intimate hammock. 'I used to think you were the best dancer.'

César didn't answer her right away, and she found herself tensing in his arms. She had never danced with him, but she could remember watching him. Or had it been another man she had watched?

'If you thought I was good, the others must have been pretty bad,' he replied with a scoffing laugh, shifting so that he faced her. His fingers drifted over her face caressingly, then his lips burned briefly against hers. 'Let's not think of how we were eight years ago,' he told her, his voice a low seductive murmur. 'Let's think of how we are now, here, together at last.'

'You . . . you don't remember the disco, do you?' she whispered. 'Perhaps you don't remember it because you were never there and never danced there.'

Did he stiffen? She couldn't be sure. If he did, the tension was momentary, for the next instant he was asking her, 'Does it really matter if I remember or not? Isn't this moment much more interesting and exciting? We are made for each other, *querida*. You are the only woman I have ever loved like this, the only woman I have ever wanted to be mine for ever.'

'Then why did you marry . . . ' she began, but got no further, because he kissed her again. The hammock swung wildly one way and the other, but, far from detracting from the primitive blood-boiling ardour that sprang up between them as soon as he kissed her, the precariousness of that rocking bed accentuated their excitement. Convinced that she might roll off on to the veranda floor at any minute, Glenda clung to him unashamedly, grasping him anywhere she could. Laughingly he shifted until he was under her. Again the hammock rocked.

'We'll fall out!' she gasped, pressing against him, forgetting the questions she had asked and he had so adroitly avoided answering. He had parted her robe and his hands were sliding stealthily over her smooth, scented skin, curving to the swell of her breasts.

Her senses already titillated by the shower she had shared with him, as well as by the romantic surroundings—the swaying intimacy of the hammock, the warmth of the air, the silvering radiance of moonlight—she was still surprised by the flare of passion that scorched through her when she felt the hard thrust of his body below hers. Fingers digging into his shoulders, she pushed herself up and a little away from him. Moonlight glinted in his eyes as he smiled up at her before his lips brushed against her breasts.

It was like being seared by flames. Gasping at such exquisite torture, Glenda gave in to it. The need to be possessed by him and to possess him, to be joined to his glowing masculinity, blazed through her consuming caution, stifling questions and making her for the first time in her life reckless of consequences. Sighing that she loved him, she pressed against him, all the needling sensations which being close to him had aroused rushing together inside her to create a swelling knot of desire. Responding to her urgent wanton movements with more stimulating caresses, César whispered sweet words of love and encouragement to her.

When at last he entered, gently, she gasped with unexpected pleasure at the new sensations he aroused and, finding himself warmly welcome, he coaxed her slowly and with a subtle delicacy, holding back with a control born of mature experience, waiting until she was delirious with delight and urging him towards culmination.

It came then, the forceful thrust and explosion of his passion within her, dynamiting her passion in turn. Showers of sparks seem to light up her mind and there was no separation of body from soul as sensations fused with emotions. Sinking against him, her body lapped by the heat of his and soothed by the tender caresses of his fingers, she came down from the violent heights into a melting softness, a luxuriousness she had never known before because never before had she been loved as he had loved her, putting her needs before his own.

Softly they whispered to each other about how happy they were to be together at last, about how lucky it was they had met again and had been offered another chance to love each other. All doubts and suspicions were forgotten. The hammock swung. The moon smiled. The little waves on the beach below sang a sweet serenade.

CHAPTER SIX

MONKEYS chattered. A parrot squawked. Bright sunlight shone down from a clear blue sky. Water lapped at the unseen edge of the beach and the wind soughed in the palm fronds.

On the veranda the wide hammock tilted first one way and then the other as Glenda, waking suddenly, strove to sit up. She was alone and had only just woken up, thinking she had heard a woman's high and musical voice, calling out.

Glenda managed to swing her legs over the side of the hammock and she jumped down quickly to the floor of the veranda before the hammock threw her out. A memory of the night-time flashed into her mind and she smiled to herself in amusement at her own and César's antics when they had made love in the hammock. Twice they had been ejected by the precarious swinging bed and had landed in a heap on the floor. It had been a wonderful yet hilarious night of love, one she would never forget.

But someone was in the house and calling in Spanish. Pulling her robe about her, she tied the belt again and ran fingers through her tangled hair. She felt great, on top of the world, and she longed to be with César again, to go swimming with him, perhaps snorkelling, as he had promised. After she had interviewed him, of course.

She was approaching the patio doorway when

a young woman came through it. Seeing Glenda, the woman stopped in surprise, her arched black eyebrows arching more than ever, her deep brown, almost black, eyes opening wide.

'Who are you?' she demanded in Spanish. Her initial surprise over, her eyes narrowed and her generously curved poppy-red mouth curved down at the corners as her glance swept over Glenda's tangled hair, much-kissed lips and glowing cheeks, coming to rest on the curves of her white breasts just showing in the opening of the beach robe. 'And where is Rafael?' she added.

'I . . . I'm Glenda Thompson,' replied Glenda, rather nervously pushing the hair back from her brow. The woman was a few years younger than she was, about twenty-three, she thought, and was as slender and taut as a willow branch. She was dressed in a frock that Glenda could only describe as gaudy, with big red poppies splashed all over a dark green background. V-necked and long-sleeved, it clung to the woman's slim shapely figure to froth out into many frills at the calf-length hemline.

'You are *americana?*' snapped the woman. Her skin was white and her long luxuriant black hair was swept back from her forehead and hung down her back to her waist. 'Then I speak English. I am Rosario Reyes, and I am come to see Rafael to find out if he coming to the hotel this evening. It is the last night of the Easter festival and I shall be dancing there. It is my profession, the dancing.' Rosario's lips widened in a flashing charming smile and she performed a few dance steps on the veranda board, her high-heeled black shoes drumming as she raised her arms above her head, her fingers snapping in imitation of castanets. 'I am the best,' she announced with a fiery lack of modesty. 'But where is Rafael?'

'I don't know. I've just woken up and . . . '

'He was here, with you, last night,' Rosario insisted. 'You were not here alone.'

'No, not alone. But I wasn't with Rafael. I don't know Rafael,' said Glenda, wondering how much she should tell this fiercely attractive woman about César. Rosario was wearing a red hibiscus flower in her black hair as if it was the most normal thing to do, and her eyes were accentuated by layers and layers of green make-up on the lids and thick black mascara on the lashes.

'But this is Rafael's place. He live here when he is on the island.' Rosario's eyes narrowed, their expression hostile. 'You do not want me to know where he is, do you?' she accused. 'You think that because he make love to you last night he is yours. Like all northern women you think that because a man is your lover he must show no interest in any other women.'

'No, I don't think that,' said Glenda, backing away from the smaller woman. 'I wasn't here with Rafael. I don't know Rafael. I've never met Rafael.'

'So how did you come here? Who brought you here if he didn't?' said Rosario sharply. 'Ah, do not believe you can deceive me with lies,' she continued, the words hissing out through her set white teeth, her long shapely upper lip lifting in a sneer. 'You met Rafael some place and fell in love with him, persuaded him to bring you here so you could make love, so you can go back to your own country and boast of the conquest you made while you were on holiday here, laugh about it with your silly sex-starved women friends . . . '

'I did not persuade him to bring me here,' retorted Glenda, made suddenly furious by the other woman's suggestions. 'I don't know any Rafael. I came here with César Estrada, at his invitation. He and I are old friends. I knew him eight years ago in Montreal and I came here to interview him . . . '

'But César never comes here,' Rosario interrupted, surprise dispersing her jealous rage. 'Never. He likes to live in an old Spanish house in Puerto Plata when he isn't in New York. They say he has an apartment in Greenwich Village where he does all his writing. Why would César want to bring you here?' The expression of surprise gave way to one of sardonic amusement. 'Ah, I think I understand,' Rosario went on softly, and she actually winked one eye. 'He bring you here because he do not wish his wife to know about you. That figures.'

'That isn't so,' Glenda burst out defensively, but stopped as a chill swept through her at the realisation that Rosario could be right.

'Do not worry. I will tell no one,' said Rosario, smiling charmingly again. 'As long as you were not with Rafael I do not care who you were with. But if Rafael is not here, where is he, and why did he not come to the hotel last night to watch me dance? He promised he would.'

'I don't know. I've told you I don't know any Rafael,' said Glenda, thinking wryly how repetitive she was beginning to sound. 'Who is he?'

'Dr Rafael Estrada. If you know César well, as you say you do, you would know about Rafael,' taunted Rosario. 'He is César's twin brother.'

This time it seemed to Glenda that shock froze the blood in her veins. She stared at Rosario's beautiful mocking face while chaotic thoughts raced through her mind.

'His twin brother?' she managed to croak hoarsely.

'*Si.* Everyone here knows the Estrada twins,' replied Rosario lightly. 'Or knows about them, I should say. They are not identical, you know, but they are alike enough to be able to deceive people who do not know them well: the same hair, the same skin colouring. But really they are very different.' She paused to peer closely at Glenda. 'Are you all right? You have gone very pale.'

'Yes, of course I'm all right,' said Glenda quickly. 'Just a little faint from lack of food—I haven't had my breakfast yet. Let's go inside. Perhaps you'd like to have something to eat with me? Or some coffee?'

'No, I have nothing, thank you. I just want to know where Rafael is, and since you do not know I will be on my way.'

They stepped into the living-room and walked through to the kitchen. Glenda looked out through the window. There was no grey Hyundai truck parked beside the house. Instead there was a small black car.

'Is that your car?' she asked Rosario, turning into the room. The young woman was standing at the kitchen table staring down at a piece of paper that lay on top of it beside an empty coffee mug.

'It say he'll be back at noon,' Rosario murmured, still staring at the paper.

'What does?' Glenda went over to the table.

'This note. Look.' Rosario picked up the sheet of notepaper and handed it across the table. 'It is written to you, but it is not signed. Rafael write it—I recognise his writing. Yet you say you do not know him, that he was not here. You lie to me. You pretend his brother was here with you.'

'No, I swear I didn't lie. César brought me here . . . in the grey truck. A Hyundai.' Glenda looked up from the bold black scrawl on the paper with the simple message, *'Glenda, I'll be back at noon.'* She couldn't remember what César's writing had been like, so she couldn't argue with Rosario on that matter.

'Rafael drives a grey Hyundai truck,' said Rosario, and she sat down abruptly on a chair. Her head between her hands, she spat out some vicious-sounding Spanish words. Glenda got the impression that the attractive, passionate dancer regarded all men as deceivers and Rafael Estrada as the most mischievous and devious of them, a cunning devil who had broken more than one woman's heart. 'They tell me what he is like, but I do not believe them,' she moaned, and tears swam down her face. Her mascara ran too. She looked up at Glenda with piteous tear-stained eyes. 'He deceive you too. He pretend to be César. Often they have done it, I have been told, pretended to be each other, to play the practical joke. Rafael brought you here, not César. He deceive you and he deceive me too. Ah, if only he were here I would scratch his eyes out!' Again the stream of invective, mixed Spanish and Anglo-Saxon words, shocking in their virulence when they were uttered by such a pretty woman.

Slowly Glenda also sat down, remembering the medical book she had looked at the previous afternoon and the name Rafael Estrada written on the fly-leaf. The writing had been the same bold scrawl as that on the sheet of paper she held in her hand. Scrawling and almost illegible. Doctor's writing? Vainly she tried to remember if she had ever seen César's writing, if he had ever written to her. Once only, he had sent her a Christmas card. His signature had been small, neatly written, almost printed. The address on the envelope, too, had been printed neatly. Was it possible she had been tricked yesterday? And also last night? Tricked into falling in love with a stranger? She thought of the differences she had noted in the man she had presumed to be César, and looked across at the sniffing Rosario. Now she could check on those differences.

'Maybe César borrowed Rafael's truck,' she suggested coolly, 'and arranged with Rafael to borrow this house.'

'César does not drive,' replied Rosario, wiping tears from her cheeks.

'How do you know? Have you ever met him?'

'But of course I have.' Rosario was scornful. 'My eldest brother went to school with the twins. They were often at our house in Santo Domingo when I was a child. It was from my brother I learned that they play tricks on people.'

'When was the last time you saw César?'

'I am not sure. Maybe two weeks ago when he return from the States to visit his family in the capital and to attend a reception given for him by the President. Everyone is very proud of him because he write that novel and win an American award. I do not care for him as much as I care for Rafael. He is fat and lazy.'

'Fat?' Glenda felt a strange sinking in her heart.

'Sure. He must be about ten kilos heavier than Rafael and he is not quite as tall.' Rosario's eyes widened and sparkled with bright intelligence. 'It wasn't César, was it, who brought you here? You know because I tell you César is fat and doesn't drive.'

'He . . . he could have learned to drive lately,' Glenda argued weakly.

'Then why does he let his wife drive him everywhere when they visit Santo Domingo?' Rosario challenged, and clutched her head in her hands again. '*Por Dios!*' she wailed. 'I do not know whether to laugh because Rafael tricked you yesterday or to cry because he had tricked me by bringing you here and staying with you last night instead of coming to see me dance at the hotel.' Half sobbing, half laughing, Rosario buried her face in her hands.

'I feel the same,' sighed Glenda, staring down at the jet black hair with the stark white parting. But, beneath the empathy she felt with the younger woman, another emotion was rising, a spiteful desire to be revenged on the man who had tricked her into coming to this place and who had seduced her into falling in love with him. She pushed her chair back and sprang to her feet. 'I'm going to Puerto Plata right now,' she announced. 'If that's your car out there, could you drive me to Samana, and can you tell me how I can get from there to the city?'

Rosario looked up, surprise glinting in her eyes. The eyelids and the skin below her eyes were smudged green and black by her tears, and Glenda had to hold back a longing to laugh.

'But don't you want to wait here for Rafael to come back?' asked Rosario. 'Or for César, if you still think it was he who brought you here?'

'It wasn't César. The man who brought me here wasn't fat and he could drive . . . well, after a fashion he could . . . and I don't want to see him ever again,' replied Glenda tautly, picking up the note that had been written to her and tearing it up into several pieces. 'But I think you should be here when he returns.' She drew a long shaky breath. 'And when he asks where I have gone, don't say anything about my knowing he had played a trick on me. Just tell him I have gone to see César in Puerto Plata,' she added, seeing suddenly how she could be revenged on Dr Rafael Estrada. She was sure he wouldn't want his brother finding out how he had deceived her.

Rosario looked puzzled for a moment. Then, as she caught on, her eyes began to dance with merriment and she clapped her hands in delight.

'It will give me great pleasure to tell him that.' She laughed, and jumped to her feet. 'But quickly, go and get dressed and I will drive you into Samana. There will be a *público* bus leaving the wharf soon for Puerto Plata.'

Fifteen minutes later, Glenda sat in the front

of the small black car next to Rosario as they
drove along the lane to the main road. Her
suitcase and shopping bag were stowed in the
back seat and she was eating a banana, the only
breakfast she had been able to grab.

She didn't look at the pretty seaside house
where she had stayed for two nights, but regret
for what had happened there had already begun
to gnaw at her. She had been deceived. No, that
was wrong. She had let herself be deceived by a
man who had seemed to resemble the César
Estrada she had believed she had remembered.
She realised now that she had romanticised her
memories of César and that the man she had met
in the market the day before yesterday had,
except for a few small discrepancies, fleshed out
her fantasy, been the realisation of her vague
romantic dreams. He had made her romancing
come true. Starved for love, she had responded
willingly to his passionate overtures, recklessly
ignoring the warnings and suspicions that had
occasionally surfaced her mind, letting her heart
rule her head for once.

How easily he had duped her! What a fool he
had made of her. How he must be laughing at
her now, at her confessions of love for him, at
her complete capitulation to his lovemaking,
regardless of the consequences. The white buildings of Samana, dazzling in the bright sunlight,
blurred before her as unusual tears filled her eyes,
tears of regret mingling with tears of mortifica-
tion because she had behaved no differently than
a romantic innocent teenager might have behaved,
letting herself be led astray by a practised deceiver

and seducer. She glanced sideways at Rosario's perfect profile.

'How long have you been in love with Rafael?' she asked curiously.

'Since I was sixteen I have wanted him to be my husband,' confessed the dancer. 'But he went away to the States to become a doctor and when he come back he say he is not ready for marriage, that he want to do more training to be a specialist of some sort—I do not know what.' Rosario shrugged her shoulders. 'So he go away again to the States, coming back only in the summer months to do voluntary work here in the peninsula at the poor people's clinics. That is what he is doing now.' She sighed. 'But when he finished his training he did not come back here right away. He went to Central America to be a doctor to poor people there. Me, I think he is nuts to want to do work like that when he could earn much money treating rich people.'

'But you still want to marry him?' asked Glenda. They were approaching the wharf. In the bay the blue water leapt and glittered and the moored sailing boats bobbed. The two Canadian boats were still there, their flags snapping in the brisk breeze.

'Yes, I do. That is why I am so glad you have decided to leave,' said Rosario. She guided the car into the kerb, parking it behind another vehicle. She turned off the engine and slanted a dark provocative glance at Glenda, her lips curving in a malicious smile. 'I like you, but I don't want you to stay around. I can see why Rafael finds you attractive and a challenge. You're pretty and kind-looking, yet you're cool

too, and not easily impressed by masculine
charmers. Rafael would want to conquer you. I
guess he tried last night and liked it. That is why
he left a note for you saying he would be back.
He wants to do it with you again.' She laughed,
a mocking trill. 'He'll be one mad *hombre* when
he returns to his house and you are not there,
and I will have the chance to comfort him, to
offer myself in your place. But come quickly, the
público is waiting. There.'

As soon as Glenda and Rosario stepped out of
the car, children of all ages, sizes and colour
crowded around them offering twists of brown
paper containing tiny golden brown peanuts and
demanding dimes. Rosario shooed them away
with a few sharp words, but Glenda stopped to
delve into her purse for dimes. She accepted
several twists of paper.

'The bus is leaving.' Rosario grabbed Glenda's
arm and pulled her towards the vehicle. 'And it's
full. You'll have to stand. *Adiós,* Glenda. I hope
we never meet again.'

Hampered by her heavy case and the big canvas
bag, Glenda struggled up the steps. The stern-
eyed, dark-faced driver demanded payment at
once and she had to put down the case while she
found the correct number of *pesos*. As she paid
him, she was aware that the crowd of people on
the bus had stopped chattering to stare at her,
and when she turned after paying she found
herself being looked at by many pairs of alien
eyes.

The bus doors swished closed. The vehicle
moved with a jerk away from the kerb. Glenda,
in danger of losing her balance, grabbed hold of

the corner of the back of the nearest seat, and
her case fell against her legs. The bus picked up
speed along the boulevard and everyone began
to relax and talk again. At the back somewhere
hens cackled in a wire cage.

Then there was a movement in the aisle.
Someone was coming along it from the back,
pushing through the double row of passengers
standing in it. The bus lurched round the curve
in the road, leaving the boulevard behind and
surging past the market and shopping centre. The
person who had struggled along the aisle appeared
and grinned at Glenda.

'Hi, ma'am,' said Alberto. 'I take you to a seat
at the back. I take your case too. Where you go?
Puerto Plata?'

Never in her life had she been so glad to see a
familiar face, thought Glenda as she pushed and
shoved after him with many apologies and thank-
yous. Yet no one seemed to mind having to make
room for her to pass. Mostly young people in a
party mood for the Festival, they grinned at her,
said often, 'No problem', and some even introduced themselves by name. At last she reached
the empty seat which was being guarded jealously
by a friend of Alberto. It was next to a huge
black woman who was nursing the cage of hens.

Glenda sat down gratefully and Alberto, her
case between his legs, stood beside her. She held
the canvas bag on her knees. The bus left the
main highway and began the climb into the
mountains.

'Many people on bus going home to their
farms, so it stop often to let them off and take
on more going to the Carnival in the city,' Alberto

explained to her. 'It take many hours for us to get there.'

'How long?'

'Oh, about four hours. We'll be there before dark' His dark eyes studied her curiously. 'Why you not wait for Dr Estrada to come back?' he asked.

If she had had any doubts about the identity of the man who had invited her to stay with him in Samana, they were now gone. Alberto knew him as Dr Estrada, called him by that name without hesitation. Dr Estrada who would help him to get to university; Dr Estrada who was not married because he preferred to work among the poor people of his country.

'How do you know he asked me to wait for him to return?' she countered, not wanting to lie to Alberto yet not wanting him to know all her business either.

'I know because he write a note for you when I went to get him to come to see my grandmother who was taken ill during the night,' replied Alberto. 'Why you leave before he come back?'

'I have things to do in Puerto Plata today, before I leave to go to Canada tomorrow.'

He nodded as if understanding and said, 'I hope you leave note for him saying where you gone. He'll worry about you if you haven't.'

Biting her lip, Glenda looked away from him, across the ample bosom of the big black woman and out of the window at the thick rain forest that edged the climbing, twisting road. She hadn't left a note. She had left Rosario instead to tell César . . . No, no, he wasn't César. He was Rafael, leaner and taller than César, who could drive—after a fashion. The bus reached the crest of the hill, seemed to hang there for a moment, then plunged down the other side, rattling and lurching. The hens in the cage squawked and fluttered. The young people standing in the aisle fell against each other, laughing. Alberto swung against Glenda and apologised, grinning all over his face.

'It's OK,' she said, smiling back at him.'Tell me what is wrong with your grandmother.'

'She have a pain here, often.' Alberto poked a thumb at his stomach. 'Last night it was very bad and she spit up blood and I have to come for Dr Estrada. He say he think it is an ulcer. This morning, early, he come for her and drive her to the hospital for an operation.

At this point the black woman joined in the conversation, asking Alberto sharp questions in the old-fashioned, limited English of the peninsula. The name Estrada came up often. Glenda looked at Alberto enquiringly.

'What is she saying?' he whispered.

'She saying she know Dr Estrada. She say he very good doctor, very kind. He save her daughter's life when baby giving trouble being born. She say she proud to know us because we know him. She say he will do his best for my grandmother.'

Glenda turned to the woman, who introduced herself as Victoria Jones and offered a big, pale-palmed hand. Glenda shook the hand and offered her own name.

'You *yanqui?*' asked Victoria.

'No, Canadian.

The woman looked puzzled so Alberto

explained. The woman nodded and smiled some more and went off into a stream of words. Alberto interpreted again.

'She say you very welcome in this country. All Canadians welcome and come often to hotel in Samana, spend much money. They also have big bank in Puerto Plata,' he explained.

The bus lurched to a stop in a village of small huts. There was much shoving and pushing and shouting as some villagers left the bus and others boarded it. The seat behind Glenda was empty, so Alberto and his friend sat down and there was no more conversation. The bus started up again and clanked around some more hairpin bends, climbing up on a sort of plateau across which the road ran straight past small farms where coconut husks were being burned, blurring the scenery with drifts of pale bluish smoke.

Glenda closed her eyes, leaned her head against the back of the seat and thought of Rafael Estrada. Why had he done it? Why had he pretended to be his brother? For sheer mischief, or for kicks? Had it given him some sort of perverted sexual thrill to seduce a woman who believed him to be his brother? And how could a man like him, a respected and revered doctor of medicine, play such an unkind trick?

Memories of how he had cared for her during the first night she had been at the house at Samana stormed suddenly into her mind. If she had not been so ill and had had her wits about her, surely she would have questioned then how it was that César could be so cool and practical when he had a sick, helpless woman on his hands? She would have wondered why he had gone on about hepatitis being so rife amongst the poor people; if she had questioned him, would he have admitted then that he wasn't César Estrada, the writer, but Rafael Estrada, the doctor? And most important of all, would he have made love to her last night?

Would she have let him if she had known for certan he wasn't César? She remembered again her doubts and suspicions about him while he had been gone—presumably to attend to Alberto's grandmother—how she had laughed at them, pushed them away from her. Now she could see why she had done that. She had wanted him to make love to her, so she hadn't questioned him in case she had destroyed the spell he had cast over her.

The bus stopped, and the black woman asked to be let out. After a lot of shoving and pushing the woman managed to get through the crowd with her cage of hens. Glenda slid over to the window and Alberto came to sit beside her. The bus took on more passengers and started up again. It was stiflingly hot, the air foetid even though all the windows were wide open. Green and gold under the arch of a brilliant blue sky, the beautiful scenery rolled by, long vistas of hillsides covered with rain forest sliding down to the sun-dazzled Caribbean Sea on one hand, long rugged mountain ranges guarding lush valleys on the other.

'Where you want to get off in Puerto Plata?' asked Alberto. He had to raise his voice for her to hear him above the noise of the bus roaring in through the open window and the sound of many voices singing and chattering.

'I am going to the house of César Estrada.
You know where that is?' she replied.

'Sure. We get off bus in the Boulevard and I
go with you, show you the way, carry your case
for you,' he replied with a simple sweet chivalry
that touched her heart. In spite of the smells, the
heat and the noise, she wouldn't have missed this
bus ride for anything, Glenda thought. Only by
travelling like this had she come closer to the real
people of the country, discovered their innate
warmth and friendliness.

'Have you ever met César Estrada?' she asked.

'No, he does not come to Samana. You know
him, ma'am?' replied Alberto politely.

'Yes. At least I used to know him once, years
ago.'

'He write very good book. It sell many copies,
make him much money. He is famous now, the
doctor tells me, and live mostly in New York. He
comes only for the vacation to this country. He
will be in Puerto Plata now for Easter.' Alberto
nodded wisely as if he was in César's confidence.
'I know because Dr Estrada say his brother at
home for a few weeks.'

Well, at least something fitted in with the
information Glenda had received from the housekeeper at César's house when she had called
earlier in the week. César was at home. He would
be at the house when she called later this afternoon, if she ever survived this journey, and she
would be able to interview him. She looked into
her canvas bag to search for a handkerchief in
her handbag and also to check that she had her
tape-recorder. She found the handkerchief but
not the recorder. With a groan she realised she

hadn't seen it since she had picked it up from the
deck last night and had put it on the table. It
was still at the house by the sea.

'You all right, ma'am?' asked Alberto, looking
at her anxiously. 'It's very hot.'

'Yes, I'm all right. I've just found out I've left
something at Dr Estrada's house. Maybe you saw
it last night when you cleared the table on the
deck? A tape-recorder?'

'*Sí,*I find it. I put it in the kitchen. You not see
it there this morning?'

She hadn't noticed. She hadn't thought about
it. She had been too confused by Rosario's arrival,
and the discovery that the man she had been
staying with was not César, to even think about
the tape-recorder.

'No, I didn't see it,' she sighed.

'Don't worry. When the doctor finds it he will
send it to you, or follow you to his brother's
house to give it to you. When you leave our
country, ma'am?'

'Tomorrow morning.'

'I wish I could come with you to Canada.'

'You wouldn't wish that if you'd ever lived in
Canada for a winter,' she told him. 'It gets very
cold there. And there are no palm trees.'

'I know that. But there is work and much good
baseball,' he replied serenely. 'One day I come.
You give me your address, ma'am, so I can visit
you?'

'Oh, of course.' Glenda took out her notebook,
ripped a piece of paper off, and printed her
address and telephone number on it. 'And if you
find the tape-recorder you can tell Dr Estrada

where to send it,' she said. 'Will you do that for me, Alberto?'

'With pleasure, ma'am. No problem.' He took the paper from her and laboriously read out the address, asking, 'I say it right?'

'Sounds good to me,' she said.

He put the piece of paper away in a wallet he took out of his back pocket, and Glenda looked out of the window beside her again. Talk about the tape-recorder had dredged up a memory of the previous evening, when the instrument had been swept from the table to the floor of the deck by a man's violent hand. It was from that moment that everything had got out of hand, she realised, and yet it was then she should have made a stand and hounded him with questions about himself, tricked him into confessing he was not the man she had once known in Montreal.

Instead he had begun to romance her, speaking to her softly, wooing her with smouldering glances, suggesting that they have the affair they had never been able to have eight years ago. True, he had given her some information about himself for her notes, but, except for him having been pestered by interviewers, everything he had told her had concerned only family background which had been the same for him as for César, and as soon as she had begun to press him he had refused to be interviewed, postponing it to the next day.

Oh, she should have seen through him—but she hadn't. Even when she had tried to escape from him, she hadn't run because she had guessed he wasn't César. She had run into the house away from him because she had been in danger of surrendering to his undeniable attractions. She had tried to escape from her own desire.

He had romanced her, blinding her to reality, and she had truly believed she had at last found her true mate. She had welcomed his body into hers and had experienced a satisfying consummation of passion which could only have happened if they truly loved each other, couldn't it?

As the miles went by and the bus trundled down from the mountain road and on to the fast highway to Puerto Plata, the question remained unanswered. Aching with regret for what had happened between herself and Rafael Estrada, because it had been nothing more than a game for him—a game at which he was expert at knowing how to control every move—Glenda sat silent and morose, puzzling over her own behaviour.

CHAPTER SEVEN

THE sun was a ball of fire low in the sky when the *público* at last swept into the long Boulevard of the city, and the excitement of the young people on the bus at having almost arrived at their destination communicated itself to Glenda, penetrating through her abject lethargy. The sides of the wide street were thronged with people of both sexes, most of them youths and girls, all dressed up in their best clothes.

They were collecting in that street, Alberto told her, for the dancing and singing that would take place that night, and also to buy sweetmeats from the many stalls that had been set up, and to be entertained at sideshows.

'We are poor, but we know how to enjoy ourselves,' stated Alberto. 'And there will be no trouble here. Everyone will behave. If anyone doesn't the police come quick to take him or her away, to lock them up for the night. See there, policemen in the crowd with walkie-talkies. When they see someone fighting or causing trouble, they call on their walkie-talkies and, in a snap of a finger, the police truck comes to take the troublemakers away. The Republic's police are efficient, very fast. That's why we have no riots, no problems.'

His enthusiasm for the speed and efficiency of the police force chilled Glenda momentarily and she guessed that a certain brutality went hand-in-hand with the police force's quick reaction to troublemakers, but there was no time to ponder the matter and ask questions, because the bus had stopped and Alberto was urging her to follow him along the aisle to the door.

After arranging to meet his friend at that same place in half an hour, Alberto urged Glenda to follow him across a piece of waste land and up a hill to the end of a cul-de-sac of little old houses, not much more than shacks. From that narrow road they walked into a street Glenda recognised. It was lined with bigger houses, most of them Victorian in design with high gables and wide verandas. Within a few minutes they were standing outside the house of César Estrada. It was three storeys high and its concrete blocks were painted brown. The fretwork decorating its gable and its veranda was painted cream.

They went up the steps to the imposing double front door. Alberto put down her case.

'I go now, ma'am,' he said.

Glenda groped in her purse, pulled out a handful of *peso* notes and handed them to him.

'Thank you, Alberto. You've been a great help. Goodbye.'

'Thank you, ma'am, thank you very much.' Alberto's big eyes shone as he looked at the fistful of *peso* notes. 'You come back pretty soon to this country.'

He skipped down the steps and ran off down the street. For a few moments Glenda stood quietly, composing herself, preparing in her mind what she would say in Spanish when the house-keeper opened the door. The street was quiet. No traffic passed along it. On the opposite side, the white façades of the houses glowed pink in the last rays of the sun. Shadows deepened where she was standing and the sound of music—thrumming guitars and the erotic beat of drums—welled up from the Boulevard, giving the encroaching dusk an enchantment, reminding her of the previous night when she had lain in a man's arms, in a swinging hammock . . .

Impatiently she turned and pressed her thumb against the bell-push, heard chimes peal inside. Lights were coming on in the houses now, the windows brimming with yellow and pink. Faintly across the street she could just make out the outline of a grey truck parked negligently half on and half off the pavement. Was it a Hyundai? Her pulses leapt. The door behind her opened, and she turned.

The wrinkled walnut-coloured face of the housekeeper softened into a smile of recognition.

'*Buenas noches, señorita,*' she said.

'Señor César Estrada? Is he at home?' queried Glenda.

'*Sí, señorita.* Please come in.'

Picking up her suitcase, Glenda walked past the woman and into the vestibule. The door was closed and the housekeeper led her through the inside door into a hallway, a foyer that ran the width of the house, from side to side rather than from front to back.

'Please wait here,' said the housekeeper politely. 'I go tell Señor César you are here.'

She went off in the direction of a stairway that was at one end of the hallway. A magnificent balustrade of carved wood curved beside the

stairs, disappearing upwards to the next floor.
Putting down her case, Glenda looked about her
with interest. The walls of the hallway were
panelled in golden wood and the high ceiling was
decorated around the edges with carved roses. In
the centre of the ceiling was a painting of nude
cherubs flying about. Glenda's glance came down
to the tiled floor, a mosaic of coloured slate laid
in a geometric design. Up from the floor, her
gaze lifted to an antique chair made from reddish
mahogany, and on the back of which was carved
the figure of a man in armour, holding a sword
in his hand. On the seat of the chair was a man's
white sunhat, high-crowned and broad-brimmed.
Glenda was staring at the familiar-looking hat
when a woman spoke behind her.

'Who are you, and what do you want?'

The Spanish was accented and the emphasis in
all the wrong places, destroying the lilting melody
of the language, giving it a guttural edge. Glenda
turned quickly. Just inside one of the glass door-
ways in the wall opposite to the vestibule stood
a woman whom she judged to be a few years
older than herself.

Shoulder-length hair, obviously lightened to
blonde by a rinse, hung about a long thin face in
which pale blue eyes, enlarged by contact lenses,
stared truculently from under thinly plucked
eyebrows. Beside the woman stood a girl of about
six years. Her hair was dark but streaked with
sand-coloured strands. Her dark brown eyes
blinked curiously at Glenda before she hid her
face shyly in her mother's skirt.

'I'm Glenda Thompson, from Canada. I've
come to see Señor César Estrada.' Glenda spoke

English, sure that she would be understood. She spoke pleasantly and smiled, so she was unprepared for the woman's rude reaction.

'You dare to come here?' the woman snapped in English, and Glenda recognised at once an accent similar to her own.

Ice-blue eyes glaring, the woman advanced and the little girl turned and ran through the open glass doorway on to a garden patio where trees were already merely shadows.

'Go away,' ordered the woman coldly. 'César doesn't want you here. Nor do I. Get out right now, or I'll call the police.'

'But I'm an old friend of César's. I knew him years ago in Montreal,' Glenda replied calmly, not giving an inch. She had dealt with much fiercer opposition in her time and now she was so close to meeting César again, and to interviewing him, she was determined to hold her ground.

'I know who you are, what you are and why you've come here, and I'm telling you to get out. I have every right to ask you to leave. This is my home. I'm Janice Estrada, César's wife.'

'I'm so pleased to meet you.' Ignoring the hostility that was glaring at her from Janice's pale eyes, Glenda held out her hand.

'Get out! Go away!' An ugly red colour staining her neck, Janice knocked Glenda's hand down. 'Go back to Canada and leave César and me alone!'

'But I'd like to see him just once before I go. I'm leaving tomorrow morning, so you needn't worry about me hanging around and pestering you. Please, let me see him,' Glenda persisted.

She had heard footsteps on the stairs at the end of the hallway and the sound of a man's voice. Soon César would appear and she would be rescued from this woman's fierce hostility.

'Get out! Go on, before I hit you!' Janice shrilled, and raised a hand as if to strike at Glenda's face. Glenda backed away and collided with her suitcase for a second time. It seemed to her that Janice was psychologically unbalanced, and she wondered why.

'Ah, *querida,* at last you arrive. The journey by bus wasn't too uncomfortable for you, I hope?'

Astounded by the sound of the deep voice that had seduced her with endearments during the night and was now greeting her in a light mocking way, Glenda turned sharply. Two men were approaching her and Janice from the stairs; two men the same and yet not the same. Both were wearing white trousers and white shirts. Both had rough sand-coloured hair springing back from their foreheads. Both had olive-coloured skin. Both possessed aristocratic Spanish features—high-bridged, haughty noses and thin, sensually curling lips.

One of them, the one who was slightly in front of the other—he would always be the leader, she guessed—was a little taller than the other, as lean as a hunting cat. The other was more rounded and was actually developing a paunch. He was wearing dark-rimmed glasses. Through the lenses his eyes, slightly darker than his brother's, smiled shyly at her. She had no doubt that he was the father of the little girl who had been with Janice.

Her hands were gripped suddenly by two lean strong hands. Her tormentor was before her and pulling her forward. His cheek, slightly bristly, rested against hers in greeting and he whispered.

'For César's sake, follow my lead. Janice is out of her mind with jealousy of any woman who looks at him or speaks to him. Let her believe you're my latest lover and everything will be all right. It shouldn't be hard for you to do after last night. I'll explain later. The name is Rafael.'

'I know that, you devil,' she began furiously, but speech was cut off as his mouth covered hers in a hard smothering kiss. It didn't last long, yet it left her breathless and unable to protest further. An arm around her waist, he turned her towards César.

'You remember Glenda, César, whom we both knew in Montreal?' Rafael said smoothly. 'She's been staying with me for the last two days at Samana.'

'I remember. Hello, Glenda. It's good to see you again.' César spoke slowly and soberly, frowning a little as if he was repeating words he had been told to say, and he didn't hold out his hand to her.

'You both knew her in Montreal?' Janice, who had been watching Rafael's performance in a stupefied silence, spoke up sharply. 'I didn't know you'd ever been in Montreal, Rafael. I thought you studied medicine in the States.'

'So I did. But I used to visit César when he was in Montreal, and there I met Glenda. We had good times together, didn't we, *querida*?'

'I . . . er . . . yes. But I really hoped to see César too, when I came here,' Glenda stammered.

'To congratulate him, of course, on his novel,'

Rafael was quick to point out to the suspicious Janice.

'That's right.' Glenda managed to free herself from Rafael's arm and she stepped towards César. 'It's great to see you again.' She smiled up at him, yet felt puzzled. She had known this man in Montreal, hadn't she? But hadn't she also known the other man, the one who was standing just behind her, too? 'I've called to see you almost every day since I arrived here,' she went on. 'I left a message for you. Did you get it?'

'A message?' César frowned heavily.

'I left it with the housekeeper on Wednesday when I called. She told me she expected you to be home on Wednesday evening,' she explained. 'I left my name and the address of the hotel where I was staying. I hoped you'd get in touch with me there and I called again on Thursday morning. The housekeeper said you had returned but had gone out . . . '

'Did you get her message, César?' demanded Janice. She stood close to him, her arm linked in his possessively.

César looked uncomfortable. Sweat started on his brow and his eyes slithered from Glenda's face, at which he had been staring as if fascinated, to his brother's. With a flash of insight, Glenda realised he had received her message but hadn't told Janice about it because he had been afraid of her reaction when she found out another woman had been calling on him. Glenda decided not to pursue the subject any further, realising it would embarrass him.

'Oh, well, it doesn't matter if you didn't get it,' she said lightly, shrugging her shoulders. 'I guess your housekeeper didn't understand my Spanish. And it's turned out all right in the end, hasn't it? I've had this chance of meeting you again and . . . '

'How did you know we would be back in Puerto Plata? Where did you find out we'd returned to the Republic?' snapped Janice, still bristling with suspicion. 'Did you tell her, Rafael?'

'Not guilty,' he replied.

'No one told me,' said Glenda. 'I just hoped César would be here. When I knew I was going to come here on holiday I remembered César saying to me once that I should call on him if ever I was in this country.' She smiled at César again. He was staring at her again in a puzzled way while he chewed nervously at one corner of his lower lip. 'Don't you remember inviting me?' she asked.

'Glenda. *Querida.*' Rafael spoke softly. His hand was on her arm. 'You've done what you wanted to do, you've met César again. Now let's go. I'll drive you back to your hotel.'

'Not yet.' She pulled her arm free of his grasp. 'I'd like to interview you, César, for the magazine I write for. All your Canadian friends and acquaintances will be so pleased to read about you. I was talking to Professor Redman just before I left Canada. He's thrilled by your success and feels he had a hand in the creation of your novel because he taught you about creative writing in English. Would you mind if we had half an hour alone together to discuss your book? I'd like to ask you some questions.'

'No.' It was Janice who answered in a brusque cold tone. 'César has been interviewed enough.

We are both tired of interviewers, of parasites like you who make their living writing about the private lives of people like César. Go away—go with Rafael. Let him take you away.'

'But it won't take long. And I won't be asking questions about your private life, only about the novel and why you decided to write it.' Glenda looked appealingly at César and saw him chew even harder at his lip, his eyes desperately avoiding hers.

'The book speaks for itself,' said Janice, who seemed to have become his spokesperson. 'César doesn't need to explain why he wrote it to you or to anyone else. Now go away.'

'I'm sorry, Glenda.' César seemed to come to life at last and she noticed how differently he spoke from Rafael—hesitantly and with much more of a Spanish accent. 'Janice is right—I have had enough of being interviewed. I think it best, too, if you go with Rafael.' His glance returned to her, seemed to plead with her for understanding.

'I'm sorry too,' she said, withdrawing with all the dignity she could muster. 'I didn't mean to intrude. Goodbye, César. Goodbye, Señora Estrada.'

'Goodbye,' said Janice in a tone that said 'good riddance'.

'Goodbye.' César looked sorrowful. 'I hope you have a good trip home.'

Arm in arm, he and Janice turned away and went out into the garden.

'If you had waited for me to return at lunch-time as I asked you to, you could have avoided this unpleasant scene,' said Rafael drily.

Glenda whirled round to face him. His broad-brimmed hat in one hand, her suitcase in the other, he was looking at her, a sardonic twist to his lips.

'Cheat! Liar!' she spat at him, giving vent at last to mixed and violent emotions that were churning inside her, striking out to hurt him, the person who had hurt her most in this farce of mistaken identity in which she had been trapped. 'You were never in Montreal eight years ago!'

'Yes, I was. But you never noticed the difference between me and César then. You were too busy being in love with Greg. You were too afraid of passion and your own sexuality to admit you wanted me, then . . . ' He broke off with a frown and pulled his hat on his head. 'I'd prefer to explain somewhere else,' he added, glancing warily at the doorway through which Janice and César had gone. 'Somewhere where Janice isn't.' He looked back at her, his glance cool, his face set in hard lines. 'Let's go and have some dinner together. I haven't eaten since breakfast, a long time ago. When I got back to my house at noon and found out from Rosario where you'd gone, I set out to follow you straight away. I hoped to get here before you did.' His lips slanted in a sardonic grin. 'I only just made it. You must be hungry too.'

She was. She was weak from hunger, even a little lightheaded. But she wasn't only hungry. She was also bewildered and unhappy because this man had lied to her, pretending to feelings he didn't have, and because *he* was the César she had remembered, not the man who married Janice.

'Why? Why did you do it? Why did you pretend to be César?' she whispered.

'To help him. That is why I've always done it. I am the firstborn. He only just survived birth and needed a lot of cossetting by my mother to survive. She asked me to watch out for him when we went to school, and I've been doing it ever since. In this case to help him mend his nearly broken marriage. In Montreal to help him out of another hole he had dug for himself through his own inability to refuse anyone, through his desire always to please others. He's always been incapable of deliberately hurting a person, so he has often ended up hurting the one person he should not be hurting.' A savage roughness hardened his voice and he frowned. 'But I can't tell you what he has done to Janice here. And it's best that she doesn't know how often I've pretended to be César to rescue him from difficult situations. Come and have some dinner with me, *por favor*, Glenda, and I'll explain what I should have explained before. Possibly, when you know all, you'll forgive me.'

Deep voice, smouldering eyes, seducing her again. Then he had gone, moving purposefully towards the vestibule, carrying her case, giving her no time to refuse to go with him. She hurried after him, following him out of the front door and down the steps.

He strode without hesitation across to the truck parked on the other side. She couldn't follow him right away because two cars passed along the street and she had to wait. By the time she did reach the truck, her case was in the back, Rafael was in the driver's seat, the engine was

going and the lights were on. He looked at her
through the open window beside him as she
approached.

'I don't want to have dinner with you,' she
snarled. 'I don't want to see you ever again or
have to listen to your lies. I think you're despic-
able, and I'm going back to the hotel.'

'How?' he asked coolly.

'I'll find a taxi somewhere.' A car went by fast
and she had to press against the door of the truck
to avoid being hit. Rafael's face wafted across
her cheeks when he spoke, she was so close to
him.

'Fool! You'll be killed if you go on standing
there. Get in and I'll drive you to the hotel, if
you must go there. By the time we get there
they'll have stopped serving dinner.' Another car
swished close to her, its horn blaring. 'Glenda,
get in!' he roared at her.

She ran round the front of the truck to the
other side. The door was already swinging open
for her, and she climbed into the seat beside him.
The truck shot forward, executed a wild U-turn
and hurtled down the street.

'We will eat first and then go to the hotel,'
announced Rafael arrogantly, now that he had
got his own way.

The truck swerved to avoid other vehicles. It
was like slaloming down a ski-run, thought
Glenda as she held on to the door with her
fingertips. Suddenly she had a flashback, to a ski-
run near Quebec City, of skiing down it with
Greg and César. César had been learning to ski
and had fallen. She had gone back to see if he
had been all right. Laughingly he had pulled her

down beside him, behaving in a way he had never behaved before, tumbling her in the snow, teasing her, kissing her. Hours later they had arrived back at the ski-lodge where a group of them, all students, had rented two rooms for the long weekend. It had been one of those times when she had felt most attracted to César and had wished she hadn't been engaged to marry Greg. Now she realised the man who had been with her that weekend had not been César, but Rafael.

The truck leapt an intersection, careered down a narrow street towards the harbour and stopped with a screech of brakes outside two old houses between which a narrow alley, lit by lantern-shaped lamps, led to the back gardens.

'When?' she asked, turning to him. 'When were you in Montreal pretending to be César?'

'Do you remember the trip to Quebec City for the end of the Carnival week there, in February?' He said, and laughed an infectious chuckle of derision. 'I was the guy who wasn't too good on skis. For once in my life I was no better than César at a sport.' He reached out and lifted her right hand from her lap, raising it to his lips. 'It was then I fell in love for the first and only time of my life,' he murmured.

'Please don't lie any more. Please,' she muttered in anguish, and snatched her hands from his grasp.

He made no reply. Opening the door on his side, he got out.

The door slammed shut. Alone in the light-splintered gloom for a few minutes, Glenda shook and shuddered in the aftermath of the evening's dramatic events, the lights on the harbour build-

ings blurring before her eyes. She felt awful, as if
she had been physically as well as mentally
abused. The door beside her opened, but she
didn't turn. Long fingers closed about her left
arm.

'Come,' said Rafael softly. 'Let me help you.
It has been a bad day for you—for me too. We
both need a good strong drink and a well-cooked
meal, to relax and talk to each other without the
shadow of César between us. There will be no
more lies, no more pretence, I promise you.'

She succumbed to his persuasion. She was too
weak from hunger, too full of conflicting
emotions, to fight him any more. She let him help
her down from the cab and lead her into the
narrow passageway between the two old houses
and up a flight of steps that turned to the right.
At the top of the steps was a wide wooden
balcony built out from the back of the house.
Two huge palm trees grew up through the floor
and their fronds, thick and fringed, created shelter
and decoration. Many tables, covered with white
cloths and set with silver and glass were scattered
about the wide wooden boards of the floor.
Couples and groups sat at the tables drinking
and eating. A slim, dark-haired woman, dressed
in black and white, came to greet them. She
smiled with pleasure at Rafael and offered him a
cheek to be kissed.

'This is a cousin of mine, Ana-Maria
Hernandez, from Spain. She and her husband
Paco came here some years ago to show us how
to make a good restaurant,' Rafael said, intro-
ducing the woman to Glenda. 'We want a table

for two, Ana, quiet, in a corner where we can talk privately.'

'I show you. This way,' said Ana.

She led them to the far end of the balcony to a round table near the railing, screened from the rest of the diners by the drooping foliage of one of the palm trees and offering a view of the lamplit harbour and the silhouettes of the mountains, black against the starlit sky. In response to a request from Glenda, Ana showed the way to a small ladies' room and there, in a mirror above the washbasin, Glenda considered her appearance with wry humour. Not only did she look as if she'd been dragged through a hedge, she also looked as if she had been wrung out like a dishcloth, she thought, and proceeded to repair the damage.

When she returned to the table, Rafael was talking to a man with sleek black hair. He was Paco, Ana's husband, and he had brought the drinks Rafael had ordered, two tall glasses of Planter's Punch complete with slices of lime. After being introduced, Paco left them alone in the warm deep shadows and the candlelight.

'So drink up,' ordered Rafael. 'As your doctor I prescribe the Planter's Punch for you.'

'You're not my doctor,' Glenda retorted coolly.

'I was last night and the night before. I could always be yours, *querida*,'

'Please,' she whispered, not looking at him, looking anywhere but at him. 'Don't make fun. Last night for you was nothing but a game you played. You . . . you deliberately romanced me so that I wouldn't question you any more about your . . . I mean, about César's novel. I can never forgive you for doing that. You seduced me . . . '

'You were very willing to be seduced,' he sniped. 'Once we had got over the small hurdle of my marriage, everything unfolded—as it should between two people who are in love with each other.

Glenda choked and spluttered in the act of drinking some of the punch. She set down the glass quickly and gave him an angry glare.

'I am not in love with you,' she whispered furiously.

'Last night you said you were, several times. Perhaps it was you who was doing the lying, the pretending, then,' he taunted, and picking up the glass he drained it. 'Mmm, that was good. Just what I needed after a hectic day. First I had to take an old lady to hospital, then I had to chase you into town and then I had to rescue César from his wife's wrath. Help yourself to some pâté and bread.' He pointed to the dish of pâté and the basket of rolls. 'You'll soon be drunk on that punch if you don't eat something.'

'I think you're very arrogant,' she retorted haughtily, taking a roll. It was hot and soft, and when she slit it open, it foamed white and fluffy. A yellow pat of butter melted into it. She bit into it hungrily.

'You'll get used to me, over the years,' he replied coolly as he stood up, empty glass in his hand.

'Chauvinist!' she sniped at his back as he left the table and disappeared behind the drooping palm fronds.

By the time he came back carrying two more

Planter's Punches, Glenda had eaten three rolls
and butter and some pâté and had finished her
drink. The rum that spiked the punch was making
her head buzz, but otherwise she felt much better,
ready to assert herself and to protect her vulnerable emotions.

Rafael's taunting mood seemed to have passed.
His expression was morose, almost grim, as he
helped himself to a roll and he ate in silence. A
thin black girl with tightly braided hair, who was
wearing a simple shift made from coloured printed
cotton, came to the table and set a large plate
before each of them, suggesting in a soft sing-
song voice that they go to help themselves from
the buffet.

In silence they went together to the long table
arranged in front of the two long windows that
acted as doors leading into the house. The table
was loaded with food of many different kinds.
First, huge bowls of salads of various vegetables;
tomatoes, peppers, beans, chicory, lettuce, red
cabbage, cucumbers, next, roasts of meat: beef,
red and juicy, lamb, pale and firm, pork crisp
with crackling. Three slim girls, all black, all
wearing cotton shifts, carved the meat on request
and laid slices of it on the plates. Then came the
cooked vegetables: yellowish yams, roast pota-
toes, bright green peas, dark red beetroot.

Glenda heaped her plate with a mixture of
salad, beef and yams and went back to the table.
Her mouth was watering and as soon as Rafael
sat down opposite to her she began to eat.

For a long time neither of them spoke. Not
until his plate was almost empty did Rafael put
down his knife and fork, lean back in his chair

and pick up his glass of punch again.

'You didn't remember Janice when you saw her, did you?' he said, surprising her.

'No. Should I have recognised her?' she exclaimed.

'I don't know,' he replied enigmatically. 'She used to work in the library at your university when César was there, so I thought you might recognise her. But I guess she looks different now. A blonde rinse and contact lenses can easily change a woman's appearance.'

'Or a man's,' she remarked drily. 'I'm surprised you or César haven't attempted to change the colour of your hair so that you or he can't be mistaken for each other.'

'Why should we do that when it's been so much fun being mistaken for each other?' he retorted. 'But we won't be able to do it much longer. He's putting on weight, doesn't take enough exercise. We grow less like each other as we grow older and the differences in our temperaments show more.' He gave her an amber-glittered glance and added softly, 'Yet you thought I was him in the market the other morning. You had no doubts I was César Estrada. It's me, not my brother, you've remembered all these years, isn't it, Glenda?'

She had to admit reluctantly that he was right. It was him she remembered, the man who had teased and tempted her during the ski-trip and on one other weekend—at her parents' cottage in the Townships when she had invited him there just before he . . . or rather before César . . .

had left Montreal, having achieved his MA to return, so she had believed, to this country.

'Why did you do it?' she asked again. 'Why did you pretend to be him when we went to the Quebec Carnival? Did he ask you to take his place?'

'No, not really.' He drank some more punch and set the glass down. Pushing aside his now empty plate and leaning his folded arms on the table, he looked at her, his eyes steady, his mouth straight. 'It is a long story, Glenda. Perhaps you would like to get something else to eat while you listen.'

'Yes, I think I would. The food is delicious.' She stood up and, plate in hand, edged round the table and past him. 'Can I get something for you?'

'No, thanks.'

She could leave, she thought, as she made her way to the buffet table. She could put down her empty plate and walk out, collect her suitcase and canvas bag from the truck and walk up to the *plaza* to find a taxi.

But she wanted to know why Rafael had pretended to be César eight years ago as well as during the past two days. If she knew why, perhaps she wouldn't feel so wretched that he had duped her.

Rafael stood up politely when she returned to the table and remained standing until she was seated again. It was something she would always remember about him and César, she thought: their good manners. They had been brought up to respect women as persons who needed to be looked after and possibly worshipped.

'How are you feeling now?' he asked. 'Have you got over that nasty little scene with Janice? I heard her threatening to hit you. It was like her. She always makes a big scene. She was afraid of César meeting you again. Even in Montreal she was jealous of you.'

'She had no reason to be. I don't remember her at all, and César never talked about her.'

'He became involved with her before he met you, during his first year in Montreal,' Rafael explained. 'She got her claws into him.' His mouth twisted cynically.

'That's a very sexist thing to say,' Glenda objected.

'So I'm sexist about some women,' he conceded easily. 'And Janice is one of them. She made a big play for César and got him. When I flew to Montreal from Chicago that winter to visit him, I found him in one hell of a mess. Janice had just told him she was pregnant with his child and was insisting that he marry her right away and not go to Quebec City with you and your friends. He asked me to go to Quebec City in his place because he had already paid his share of the trip. I did. When I turned up at the bus station to join all of you, everyone assumed I was him. It amused me, so I went along with the idea.' He shrugged again and gave her one of his smouldering glances. 'And I found out why Janice was so afraid of you,' he added. 'She was afraid César liked you better than he liked her. She is still afraid he does.'

'But . . . but . . . he didn't. He couldn't have done,' Glenda argued. 'At least, he never showed me that he might have liked me more than any other woman. Except on that ski-trip and another time when he and I went down to my parents' place in the Townships, he never once . . . ' She became aware of what she had just said and broke off, staring at him. He looked back at her, his eyes slitted, a sardonic smile curving his lips. On the two occasions to which she had just referred she hadn't been with César, she had been with him. They were the only times she had felt sexually attracted to César, had been roused almost to passion just by being with him. 'César was always so shy, so gentle and dreamy. At least, that's how I remember *him,*' she began to explain.

'Dreamy, gentle, shy and thinking only of his writing and so easily trapped by women,' Rafael said jeeringly. 'Excuse me for a moment.' He rose to his feet again. 'I'll be right back and we'll continue this most interesting conversation about how you really feel about César.'

CHAPTER EIGHT

ALONE again, Glenda sat by candlelight. Her chin resting on her hand, her elbow on the table, she gazed at the leaping yellow flame in the glass jar. It was all coming back to her now, in a riot of confused images. She hadn't been really alone with César except on those two occasions which were vivid in her mind, she realised, and then she hadn't been with him; she had been with Rafael. Whenever she had been with César, the real César, there had always been other people around—at discos, at concerts in the Place des Arts, at hockey games in the Forum, at Hallowe'en and New Year parties during that autumn and winter when she had known him. And after the skiing trip she had hardly seen him, had assumed he had been too engrossed in writing his thesis to bother with socialising. She had seen so little of him she had almost forgotten him . . .

And then, on graduation day—she had attended the ceremony not to get her own degree —that had happened a year later—but to see friends receive theirs—when she had been leaving the hall, César had appeared before her. She could visualise him now, tall and distinctive-looking with his dark face and amber-dusted thick hair, looking at her intently, a slight smile curving his lips.

'Can we have lunch somewhere together?' he had asked, and she had been surprised.

'Long time no see,' she had joked awkwardly, not wanting him to take her for granted even though her pulses had quickened to his dark intent stare.

'I have been busy,' he had replied with a shrug, and she had understood.

They had lunched in an expensive French restaurant that had recently opened. Glenda couldn't remember what they had talked about. All she could remember now were her own feelings: excitement because he had invited her out alone, and because he had kept on looking at her with a strangely smouldering stare . . .

A movement alerted her. She came back from Montreal to the dark corner of the restaurant and looked across the table, meeting Rafael's strangely smouldering stare.

'That last time,' she murmured. 'When you came to the graduation ceremony and we had lunch and then went down to Orford . . . was it because César asked you to?'

'No. I was there to see him graduate and afterwards I saw you in the crowd quite by accident. You said, "Hello, César." I invited you to have lunch, intending to tell you who I was, but you seemed so happy to be with me thinking I was César that I was reluctant to tell you. I didn't want to spoil what was happening between us.' He paused, his lips twisting. 'You wouldn't have invited me to go to your parents' place if I'd told you I wasn't César, would you?'

'I don't know. Oh, I don't know,' she whis-

pered, her head between her hands now as she
avoided his eyes and stared down at the empty
plate before her. She tried to think back to the
restaurant in Montreal, where, she realised now,
she had begun to fall in love with him. 'Oh, I
was a fool not to realise you weren't César. You
were really so different from him, even then. You
were more . . . more . . . '

'More aggressive, more sexist, more chauvin-
istic?' he suggested mockingly when she hesitated.

'All of those,' she retorted with a little laugh,
giving him a quick glance, appreciating his self-
mockery while adding to herself, *And more hand-
some, more the person I always wanted to be my
lover.* Her cheeks glowed warmly at her silent
thoughts and she was glad of the shadows.

'Perhaps you did realise I wasn't César but
subconsciously you didn't want to spoil what was
happening, either,' he said. 'And perhaps the
same thing happened last night at Samana. You
had doubts about me, I sensed that you did. Yet
you didn't challenge me outright. Why didn't
you?'

Glenda's face was hotter than ever and she
couldn't look at him. She picked up her glass
and drank the rest of the Planter's Punch quickly.
It was sharp with rum and she knew she had
drunk too much too quickly, but the spirit gave
her the courage she needed to ignore his suggestive remarks.

The thin waitress came to take away their
plates and to ask them if they wanted dessert. If
so, they were to help themselves to the fresh fruits
and cheeses set out on the buffet table. Reprieved

momentarily by the girl's presence, Glenda leaned back in her chair and fanned her face with her serviette.

'It's very warm tonight.'

'Warm enough to sleep outside in a hammock,' said Rafael. She turned her head sharply and looked out at the harbour lights. He laughed softly. 'Did you really come to Puerto Plata hoping to interview César? Or did you come hoping to have an affair with him?' he asked.

'Of course I hoped to interview him!' Irritated by his suggestion, she spoke sharply and looked at him. 'It never entered my head to start an affair with him. I knew he was married, I'd read he was married in an American magazine, but I had no idea he'd married someone I might have known or met and who knew me. And I can't understand why Janice is jealous of me. César and I haven't even written to each other, let alone met each other, during the past eight years.'

'She's always known he liked you when he knew you in Montreal and she used to interfere even then to prevent him from going about with the group of students you went with,' he replied. 'She's extremely possessive. Women who have no sense of security or self-confidence often are possessive about their lovers or their husbands.' He glanced at her from beneath heavy brows, making her pulses leap. 'Janice knows you're more lovely than she is, more lively, more knowledgeable about the things that interest César, so she fears you have more influence with him than she has.'

'Oh, that's ridiculous! How can I have any

influence with him when I haven't see him for years?'

'She sees you as being like another woman writer, the one he's been having an affair with in New York,' he explained drily.

'César has been having an extra-marital affair?' Glenda gasped, and watched amusement flit across the dark planes of Rafael's face, briefly lighting it up.

'*Sí.*' His voice shook with laughter. 'I'm not surprised that you are surprised. I was, too, when I learned about it. And I have to say in his defence that he didn't intend to become involved with the woman. But as you have said, he is dreamy, gentle and at heart kind and generous. Easy meat for a certain sort of woman, for the sort of woman who needs a lover or a husband to bolster her ego. This woman, I forget her name, apparently flattered him, talked to him about literature and language. Like you, she was an interviewer for a magazine, wrote articles about celebrities . . . ' He paused meaningfully and Glenda drew the inference from his description of the woman immediately.

'So that was why Janice didn't want me to interview him,' she murmured.

'Exactly. When she found out about the affair in New York, Janice played hell with him and dragged him away, came here. They have come to this country to be reconciled, to restore stability to their rather shaky relationship for the sake of Janetta, their daughter, and Juan, their son. When César got your message on his return to Puerto Plata last Wednesday, he went into a panic. He hid the message from Janice because he didn't want to trigger off one of her jealous fits, but he was scared stiff you'd call again and she would answer the door. Fortunately when you did call on Thursday morning the housekeeper answered the door, and I was there with him when she came to tell him you had called. I told her to tell you he had gone to the market, hoping you would go there too. You did. I drove to the market to intercept you.' Rafael frowned, looked down at the table. 'My initial intentions were honourable,' he went on, giving her another underbrowed look. 'I was going to explain to you why César couldn't meet you. But you thought I was him and seemed so pleased to see me . . . or him . . . I couldn't say anything.' He laughed again, self-mockingly. 'It all came back to me at that moment how much I had liked you eight years ago and how much I'd wanted you then.' His glance seemed to sear her. 'So I pretended to be César again and persuaded you to go with me to Samana, taking you out of his way and hoping to get what I wanted at the same time!

'You tricked me deliberately,' she whispered, trying to rekindle her irritation with him.

'I couldn't have done if it you hadn't been so willing to be deceived,' he accused her softly. 'You guessed I wasn't César, but you couldn't bring yourself to challenge me. You got what you wanted, too, at Samana last night. And you wanted it from me, not from César.'

'No, I didn't. I didn't!' she denied fiercely. 'Oh, you're just trying to make out that what was wrong was right . . . '

'Wrong?' he interrupted her, his eyes blazing angrily. 'You think that what we did last night was wrong? What was wrong about it? We're two adults who are in love with each other. Neither of us is married to anyone else, so what was wrong in us making love?'

'It was wrong because . . . Oh, because you didn't tell me you weren't César.'

'But you wouldn't have done it with him, because he's married,' he reminded her tauntingly. 'And I'm surprised you didn't catch on when I told you that if you slept with me you wouldn't be sleeping with another woman's husband.' His mouth slanted in its sardonic grin. 'But perhaps you did. Perhaps it occurred to you then and you said to yourself, this man isn't César, but I'm not going to spoil everything now by asking him who he is, because I'm enjoying myself too much.'

'That isn't true,' she objected, but her voice was weak. There was no ring of defiance in it, nor of denial, and she couldn't look at him. She was too dismayed by his accurate analysis of her feelings and behaviour last night.

'Don't be ashamed of what we did,' he said softly. 'I wasn't romancing you, as you have accused me of doing, to stop you accusing me of not being César. Last night when I made love to you it was me, Rafael, who was doing it, feeling it, who wanted to do it with you; it was not César. I made love to you because I love you. *Te quiero*—the Spanish says it so much better. It says in one word that I love you and I want you.'

'Oh, please, stop. Don't say any more. Don't lie any more.'

'I am not lying, damn you!' he shouted suddenly, his eyes glittering with golden flames. Across the table they glared at each other. Ana-Maria appeared around the palm fronds, her fine-featured olive-skinned face expressing concern. She spoke quickly and demandingly in Spanish. Turning to her, Rafael answered in the same language, speaking laughingly. Ana's expression changed from one of concern to one of sparkling amusement.

'Ah, I understand,' she said in English, nodding at Glenda with a knowledgeable glint in her dark eyes. 'Shall I bring you some dessert? We have strawberries, fresh ones, steeped in a liqueur and topped with cream. Also good coffee.'

'Sounds good, Ana,' Rafael accepted, and the woman disappeared behind the palm leaves again. Across the table, he smiled at Glenda. 'I told her we have a lovers' quarrel,' he explained.

'But we're not lovers,' she protested. She was trying hard to retrieve her cool, to behave as a sensible woman, emotionally secure and able to survive without a man to boost her ego.

'Then what are we?' he challenged, anything but cool, his fiery passionate nature breaking through any control he might possess, his eyes flaming with candlelight as he leaned towards her. 'If we are not lovers, what are we? And what was it we did last night?' His white teeth jeered at her as he grinned mockingly. 'Are you trying to tell me that our togetherness last night meant nothing to you; that you were the one who was pretending? Was it all an act, Glenda? A pretence to deceive me?'

'No. No, it wasn't. I mean, I wasn't . . . Oh, God!' Glenda cooled hot cheeks with her palms. 'Why do you torment me like this? It was you who pretended to be César, and for that I will never forgive you. You . . . you took advantage of me!'

'You feel wronged and deceived just because you've found out the man you loved last night isn't called César,' he said in a hissing whisper. 'So imagine, if you can, how I feel, because you used me as a substitute for César. I could accuse you of taking advantage of me.'

'I didn't!' she gasped.

'No? Then whom did you kiss and touch?' he jeered. 'Which one of your phantom lovers did I substitute for, if not for César?'

'Oh!' She gasped again as if he had punched her, and tried desperately to maintain her poise. 'I don't want to discuss it any more,' she said as coldly as she could, but was immediately jolted when he laughed at her. 'I mean what I say,' she raged at him. 'I'm not making a joke.'

'So, that is fine by me,' he retorted. 'We will discuss César no more. We will start again as if there were no César, no Janice, but just us, you and me.'

Ana-Maria appeared again with a tray holding dishes of strawberries and cream, a silver coffee pot and two cups and saucers. She set them down on the table and chattered amiably about the Easter celebrations, asking them whether they intended to watch the sunrise next day and the parades to the churches. When Glenda said she wouldn't be able to watch the religious parades because she would be returning the next day to Canada, Ana-Maria expressed surprise and said to Rafael,

'You must persuade her to stay longer, *amigo*.'

'I am working on it, you can be sure of that,' he replied enigmatically. 'But she is very independent, very liberated, and puritanical too. She takes life too seriously—does not make jokes.' Across the table his eyes gleamed mockingly in response to Glenda's supercilious glare.

'Then she is good for you,' said Ana-Maria surprisingly, and with another friendly nod at Glenda she departed.

Determined not to encourage Rafael in any further discussion, Glenda picked up her dessert-spoon and dipped it into whipped cream. For a short while there was silence while they both enjoyed the dessert. Rafael poured coffee and handed her a cup and saucer. She thanked him stiffly, not looking at him. The short conversation with Ana had put her on guard. She was all prepared to resist him if he attempted to persuade her to stay longer in the country, to stay with him, possibly as his mistress . . .

'So there is just us, you and me, Glenda,' he said softly. 'We met briefly in Montreal and clicked. No, don't deny it,' he added quickly as she opened her mouth to disagree with him. 'We did. We have now met here and it has happened again, the chemical reaction, the magnetic attraction, whatever you like to call it, of me to you and you to me. We have fallen in love again and

I would like to marry you. In fact you're the only woman I have ever wanted to marry.'

This new approach, this fresh attack on her sensibility took her completely by surprise. The spoon fell from her hand straight into her dish. Cream and juice spurted up, splashing her face and blouse. She gaped at him.

'You're crazy,' she croaked hoarsely.

'I think I am too,' he said with a slanted grin. 'And until today I thought that most men who asked women to marry them were crazy.' He shrugged his shoulders. 'But I can see no other course for me to take right now. You see how serious you have made me? I love you and I want you. I would like you to be the mother of my children, and I have this gut feeling you won't be that if I don't ask you to marry me.'

The shadows, the few lights, seemed to be dancing around her. She dabbed at the splotches of cream and juice on her blouse, trying to steady her thoughts.

'But you're going to marry Rosario,' she said at last.

'What?' A swift frown darkened his face. 'Who told you that I am?'

'She did. Yesterday. She said that one day you and she are going to be married.'

'She romances.' His lips curled cynically. 'She indulges in foolish adolescent dreams. I have never talked of marriage to her or any other woman. Only to you.'

'She loves you.'

'No, she doesn't. She loves an image of me she has created. She'll marry someone, the young man Pedro who is her dancing partner. She's too young for me, and too simple,' he said. 'I want a more complex woman to be my wife. I want a woman who needs persuading, who challenges me in some way. I want you. Glenda, will you marry me?'

Her head, already buzzing with the rum in the punch and with the confused emotions this man aroused in her, reeled. The lights in the harbour danced before her eyes. The shadows cast by the palm fronds quivered in a faint breeze. She looked back at Rafael. Golden eyes gleamed at her from a dark face, a white shirt glimmered.

'How can I marry you?' she whispered. 'I hardly know you, and what I know I don't like.' Now she was hot again, her whole body glowing as if she were on fire within. Desire flamed up in her and had to be quenched quickly. 'You . . . you break promises.'

'What promises have I broken?' Rafael demanded sharply.

'You promised Rosario you would go and see her dance at the hotel in Samana last night.'

'I made no promise to her. I didn't go to see her because I was with you and there were better things to do. I have never made any promise to any woman, so I have never broken any.'

'You pretended to be César,' Glenda accused shakily.

'Don't think of him. Think of me.' He leaned towards her. 'You prefer me to him. You did in Montreal; you did last night in Samana. You do now. Admit it, *querida,* and say you'll marry me.'

She shook her head from side to side, trying

to clear it of confusion as much as refusing to do as he asked.

'I . . . I can't say that,' she whispered. 'I don't trust you, not after what has happened, and where there's no trust there can be no marriage . . . ' Her voice faltered, trailed off into silence. She couldn't look at him. There was a pain in her chest as if someone was squeezing her heart. It was hurting her to refuse him because she wanted more than anything else to cast caution aside and say yes, she would marry him. 'I'd like to go back to the hotel now,' she added dully. 'I'm tired, and we have to be up early tomorrow to go to the airport.'

'Then I'll drive you there,' he agreed smoothly. He had, much to her surprise, taken her refusal calmly. She glanced at him quickly, but he was already rising to his feet and she couldn't read the expression on his face.

Ana and Paco accompanied them to the flight of steps and urged them both to come back for another meal soon. Rafael went first down the steps. He opened the door of the truck for Glenda politely, wordlessly.

His silence continued as the truck weaved through the traffic and out on to the highway. He drove at his usual reckless speed and for a few strangely hopeful moments Glenda wondered whether he was going to drive past the turn-off to the hotel and take her to Samana again. When he did slow down and steered the truck into the narrow palm-shaded lane, she experienced a sharp stab of disappointment because he wasn't going to kidnap her and carry her off to his hideaway like a hero in some kind of romance, after all.

Moonlight struck silvery sparks from the dark moving mass of the sea. Rafael turned the truck into the parking space. Although light shafted out from the main hotel building, the place was quiet. Glenda commented on the lack of activity as Rafael lifted her suitcase out of the back of the truck.

'Everyone has probably gone into town for the last night of the Carnival,' he replied with an uninterested shrug.

'You don't have to come with me to the cabin,' she said, holding out a hand for her case.

'I prefer to come.' His smile flashed down at her. 'To see that you arrive there safely, of course,' he added lightly, and tucked his free hand in the crook of her arm.

Sand sifted into her sandals as they walked along the beach to the cabin. Waves sighed softly and leaves rustled. There was the sound of voices shouting and laughing. Some people were swimming and playing on the beach, making the most of their last night in the tropics before returning to the coolness of the northern spring to show off their sunburn and to brag of their adventures. A few lights shone out from the cabins, but the one Glenda shared with Ida was dark.

On the veranda she groped for her key, found it and inserted it in the lock. The door swung open, and she turned to Rafael. The time of parting had come. Best to get it over quickly, say goodbye with no regrets. But she couldn't think of anything to say. She didn't want to part from him, not yet. She didn't have to. He walked straight past her into the moon-dappled room, flicking on the switch by the door as he did. Light from one lamp dispersed the gloom. Glenda followed him inside. He dropped her case to the floor, swung the door shut, turned to her and, before she could say anything, grasped her shoulders, pulled her against him and covered her mouth with his.

The touch of his lips burned through her confusion and rekindled the fire of her desire for him. Her lips parted eagerly to the probing hot hardness of his tongue. Sliding her hands around his neck, she pressed her fingers among rough hair, preventing him from lifting his head even if he had wanted to lift it.

But although she responded hungrily to the dominance of his lips and the exploring urgency of his fingers as they moved over the thin stuff of her blouse, something inside her was holding back, and when he dragged his lips from hers to nibble at the curve of her throat she moaned,

'Oh, please go!'

'Not yet,' he said, raising his head to look at her with slitted glittering eyes. 'Not until I've given you something to remember me by; to remember my love for you so that you'll never forget me when you leave here. There is no more time for argument, *querida*. Time is running out, so I have to convince you in some other way.'

Lifting her easily, he carried her to the nearest bed. He laid her down on it and began to strip off his shirt. In the lamplight his sun-kissed skin glowed and the longing to touch him flamed through her. Yet still she resisted that longing, and when he came towards the bed, naked and unashamed, his desire for her blazing in his eyes, she put out her hands to push him away.

'No! Oh, go away! Ida might come in at any minute,' she protested.

Laughing, Rafael grasped both her wrists and knelt beside the bed, placing her palms against his chest. The expression on his face, on a level now with hers, was one of devilry mixed with tenderness.

'Ida won't be coming in,' he said softly, his lips close to hers.

'How do you know she won't?' she exclaimed, but made no attempt to pull her hands from his grasp, letting her fingers spread fan-wise over his hair-sprinkled skin, feeling the flame within her flaring up and melting all her resistance.

'I saw her this afternoon. I called here on my way to town, thinking you might have come here first. I met Ida again and she asked me to tell you, if I saw you, that she and the others—I guess she meant your fellow-tourists—would be out all night. They were going into town for the Carnival and then later were going up the mountain to watch the sunrise on Easter Day. She said to tell you she'll see you at breakfast time.' He bent his lips to the curve of her throat again. 'So you see, my love,' he added, 'we have all night to be together again. All night to make love without the shadow of César between us. This is me, Rafael, kissing you, Glenda. Me, Rafael, you are touching and arousing. *Por Dios,* never have I wanted so much to give myself to you!'

He pushed her back against the pillows and

slid on to the bed beside her. Possessing her lips again, he pressed against her until she could feel the hardness of his bones and the throbbing thrust of his desire through her clothing. She breathed in the hot male scent of him and her senses reeled wildly as excitement broke over her in long rippling waves. Hardly knowing what she was doing, she helped him slide off her clothing, and experienced an extraordinary feeling of triumph when she saw the bright glitter of combined admiration and lust in his eyes as their glance swept over her delicately tinted, silk-skinned body. Then he gathered her to him again, straining her so closely against him that they seemed fused together by the heat of passion.

Cool logic, balanced judgment, all the qualities of mind that she prided herself on possessing, were consumed by that heat. She forgot he had deceived her by pretending to be his brother. There was just him and her, their bodies and souls stripped bare of pretence at last, closely and ecstatically intimate. Overhead the fan whirred. Outside the waves sighed.

'So, do you know who I am?' Rafael demanded breathlessly as he slid over her to lie between her thighs.

'Yes, I know who you are,' she whispered, groaning a little as her body began to move rhythmically beneath the pressure of his, responding to his demands.

'Then say it, say my name,' he urged. 'Say, "I know you're Rafael and I love you".'

'I know you're Rafael and . . . and I love you. Oh, I love you dearly. Please, please . . . '

She arched against him with an urgency that surprised her, her fingernails scraping his burning skin. His fierce gasp, the hot breath entering her mouth, gave expression to her own agony of pleasure, and then he was plunging deep inside her, telling her in Spanish, the language of love, that he loved her more than any other woman he had known.

This time their fusion possessed a desperate quality, as if they were both afraid it might never happen to them again, and afterwards she held his lax, breathless body close to her while she sobbed into his shoulder.

'You believe you make love with me and not with César?' he asked gently. With a quick hot tongue he licked tears from her face.

'I believe I made love with you.'

'Good. With that I am content for now,' he murmured, and stroking her hair back from her face he kissed her again, tenderly.

She was content too, Glenda thought drowsily as a wonderful lethargy crept through her body like darkness creeps across the sunset sky. Nothing mattered except this comfortable feeling that came from knowing she was loved and was falling asleep in the arms of her lover. But she mustn't fall asleep yet. There was something she had to say before she fell asleep. She must tell him she loved him and would marry him, that she forgave him his brief, mischievous deception of her.

'Rafael,' she whispered, 'I love you.'

There was no response. With an effort she

dragged herself back from the dark abyss of sweet oblivion and added,

'I . . . I think I'd like to marry you after all.'

Her whispered words floated into the warm air and were wafted away by the whirring fan. Rafael didn't move and didn't speak. He was fast asleep.

She would tell him when he woke up, when they both woke up at sunrise, she thought hazily, and putting a possessive arm across his waist she fell down into the deep black abyss.

She dreamed that he moved, that his lips brushed her cheeks and she thought he whispered, *'Adiós, querida.'* She wanted to reply, but she was too sunk in a warm velvety darkness and she heard nothing more until Ida's rather strident voice seemed to split the darkness apart, startling her.

'Wakey, wakey, Glenda! It's morning and time we've had breakfast. Don't forget we're leaving today—in exactly two and three-quarter hours.'

Glenda sat up abruptly. She glanced around the room warily, looking for signs of Rafael having been there. Nothing. He had left nothing behind, only this feeling deep within her that the very core of her had been invaded by him and that never again would she be the woman who had come to this country to interview his brother. He had truly given her something to remember him by. Then hard on the heels of the feeling came the sharp stab of disappointment again. He had gone before she had been able to tell him that she forgave him and would like to marry him.

'Did you have a good time at the Carnival?'

she asked. Ida was busy taking clothes from the
wardrobe and jamming them into her suitcase.

'You bet!' Ida, who was tall, dark-haired and
willowy, glanced over her shoulder. 'What about
you? Did you enjoy yourself with César Estrada
at Samana? He was here again yesterday afternoon looking for you. Where did you go after
you left Samana?'

'That wasn't César,' said Glenda bluntly. Best
to tell the truth to Ida. 'That was his twin
brother, Rafael.'

'Really?' Ida's greenish eyes gleamed inquisi-
tively as she swung round. 'Had you met him
before?'

'Yes. When he visited César in Montreal.'
Glenda pushed back the sheet, swung out of bed
and, finding her thin cotton dressing-gown still in
the wardrobe, slipped it on. Ida was busy rolling
up underwear and stuffing it into a corner of her
carelessly packed suitcase.

'But you've seen César too?' she asked casually.

'Eventually,' replied Glenda, eyeing her reflec-
tion in the long mirror on the front of the
wardrobe door. Her hair tousled, her suntanned
cheeks pink, she looked different too, she thought,
as well as feeling different. She looked less serious,
less cool, her northern frostiness melted by a
tropical sun.

'Was he at Samana?'

'No, he wasn't there after all. That's why I
came back to town early yesterday. I saw him at
his house in Puerto Plata.'

'And were you able to interview him?'

'No. His wife wouldn't let me.' Glenda laughed

mockingly. 'She's the possessive, jealous type and won't let another woman near him, particularly another woman from his past.'

'What a pity.' Ida was consoling. 'About not getting the interview with him. But I bet you had a good time with Rafael at Samana.' She paused and turned to give Glenda a glinting, knowledgeable look. 'And here, last night,' she added tauntingly.

On her way into the bathroom Glenda froze in her tracks. Slowly she turned. Ida was grinning at her suggestively.

'What do you mean?' Glenda challenged.

'He . . . Rafael . . . was here last night with you,' replied Ida.

'How do you know he was?'

'I saw him leaving just as we were returning this morning. We passed his truck as it swung out of the lane and on to the highway. He went east—I guess he was going back to Samana. Why didn't you go with him?'

'I . . . er . . . Because he didn't ask me to,' Glenda snapped crossly and went into the bathroom, slamming the door after her.

But it seemed she couldn't even have a shower without remembering Rafael, because last time she had showered he had been with her, kissing her and stroking her, teaching her the delights of intimacy with him. Groaning, she turned off the shower and stepped quickly out of the cubicle to dry herself.

What was she going to do now? How was she going to forget him? In him she had found all she had ever wanted in lover and husband:

humour and compassion, strength and tenderness. So why hadn't she accepted him last night when he had proposed to her?

'He asked me too soon after I'd found out he'd deceived me,' she argued with herself. 'I'd have said yes if he hadn't tricked me into believing he was César.'

'But you knew he wasn't César,' retorted another voice within her. 'In your heart you guessed he wasn't César, even in Montreal, all those years ago. You were just afraid to challenge him in case the spell was broken, in case he stopped making love to you once he knew that you knew he wasn't César. You went along with the deception because you wanted him. You still want him. You want to stay and marry him.'

'No, I don't,' she muttered furiously to herself. 'I don't want to marry him. I've been married. I know what marriage is like, that's why I refused him really.'

'You married the wrong man. Marriage to Rafael would be different. It would be one long adventure,' said the other voice. 'Why not stay and try it?'

'Oh, shut up!' she snapped, and left the bathroom with the same haste she had entered it.

CHAPTER NINE

HALF an hour later, Glenda stood with the rest of the group of tourists from Canada in the parking lot by the main building of the hotel and watched luggage being loaded into the bus that would take them all to the airport. The sadness that she felt on leaving any place where she had enjoyed herself made her feel cold, even though the sun's rays were already hot, slanting down out of a cloudless sky.

'Best make the most of these last few minutes of warmth,' said Ida, taking off her sunhat and lifting her face to the sun. 'The latest weather news from Toronto is that spring hasn't arrived there yet, in spite of the date. There was actually a snowfall last night.' She glanced enquiringly at Glenda. 'God, you already look like a week of wet Fridays!'

'I'm sorry,' retorted Glenda stiffly and, turning away, walked towards the beach and the pounding, foaming surf. Ida's hearty cheerfulness possessed an abrasive quality she couldn't bear at that moment. Already she felt raw inside and out, raw with the longing to stay, to go over to the bus and snatch her luggage off it, to announce to the world . . . or at least to anyone who questioned her . . . that she was staying because she was in love with Rafael and wanted to marry him.

From the beach, she looked out at the sun-glittered, tumbling turquoise waves of the sea. It was this place, she thought, this beautiful island. She wouldn't be feeling regretful about leaving if she hadn't been bewitched by its golden beaches, swaying coconut palms and easygoing way of life. She would be all right once she was back in her own country and busy with her writing. Yes, that was the path to take. She must think about her career, put it first as she had when she had found out about Greg's infidelity. Her work was more important than any man. If she stayed here, if she married Rafael, she would have to give it up. She sighed heavily, admitting ruefully to herself that she would give it up without regret to marry him if only he hadn't deceived her, if only . . .

'Glen. Glen!' Ida's voice was strident, splitting the warm air. Glenda turned impatiently, sharp words rising to her lips. Why wouldn't Ida leave her alone this morning?

'What is it now?' she snapped at her approaching friend.

'There's a guy come with a message for you,' shouted Ida from the parking area, and gestured with one hand towards a slim dark-faced man who was wearing neat black trousers and a neat cream shirt.

Strange how hopeful expectation leap up in her. A message. From Rafael of course. Who else would send her a message? She hurried towards the young man.

'Are you Mees Thompson?' he asked. His thin-ness, his shining dark face and his flashing white teeth reminded her of Alberto, but she could see he was older than the boy.

'Yes, I'm Glenda Thompson.'

'Señor Estrada want to see you. He say to give you this note.'

'*Señor?*' she queried. 'Señor César Estrada?' She was aware that Ida was moving away out of earshot.

'*Si, señorita.*'

She took the note from him and, after a quick glance about her to make sure no one was watching her or taking any interest in what she was doing, she opened it. The handwriting was small and neat, not at all like Rafael's doctor's scrawl.

'Glenda,' she read silently, 'I am sorry I could not talk to you properly yesterday. Yes, I would like to be interviewed by you. Please come to my car with the bearer of this note. We will go to a place where we can talk undisturbed. Later I will take you to the airport to catch the plane. César.'

'Where is the car?' she asked, folding the note and pushing it into her skirt pocket.

'Back there.' The young man jerked his sunhatted head in the direction of the lane that led to the highway. 'It is parked under the trees. Señor Estrada not want to come here. He not want to be seen meeting you. You come with me, please, *señorita?*'

'Yes, of course I will. But I'll have to explain to my friend first.'

'I wait for you.' He nodded understandingly. 'No problem.'

Glenda went over to Ida and touched her arm. Ida turned, her eyes glinting curiously.

'Well?' she whispered. 'Is it from him? Are you going to stay here after all?'

'No, no.' Glenda shook her head. 'The note is from César. He wants me to interview him before I leave. He's waiting in a car along the lane, and he'll take me to the airport later. Will you explain to the tour guide why I'm not going with all of you on the bus? I'll see you later at the departure gate. I have my ticket. The luggage can go without me. All I need is my notebook.'

'What about your tape-recorder?'

'I left it in Samana,' said Glenda with a self-mocking grimace. 'Sheer absentmindedness.'

'Oh, sure,' jeered Ida. 'But supposing you don't turn up in time to catch the plane? How should I explain that?'

'But I will turn up—I'll make sure of that. It won't be leaving for another hour and a half and I won't take more than half an hour to interview him. I'll be at the airport in plenty of time to go through Customs and security. See you later.'

'I wonder if you will?' retorted Ida tauntingly. '*Adiós,* Glen. Send me a postcard if you decide to stay.'

More than irritated by her friend's mockery Glenda walked along the lane beside the young man and tried to remember all the questions she wanted to ask César about his novel. At last she had a chance to do what she had come to the republic to do and she wasn't going to waste one minute of this meeting with César if she could help it.

The car was long and grey and had dark smoked windows, so that she couldn't see inside but whoever was inside could see her. As she approached it, one of the rear doors swung open and César, dressed in white, of course, looked out at her. Through the lenses of his dark-rimmed glasses his eyes smiled at her a little apprehensively.

'Thank you for coming, Glenda,' he said politely. 'Please get in.'

She slid on to the warm leather-covered seat beside him. The driver shut the door.

'You came only just in time. My luggage is already on the bus,' she said.

'If I had missed you here I intended to go to the airport to find you,' he replied seriously. 'It's most important that I talk to you, Glenda.'

'The plane takes off at ten forty-five, so we have a good half-hour in which to talk. I should really be there to check in an hour before take-off, but I've warned my friend that I may be a little late.'

'I know when the plane leaves,' he replied as the car began to roll smoothly and sedately along the lane towards the highway. Riding in it was quite different from riding in the Hyundai truck.

'First I must say I hope you're not too offended about what happened yesterday,' César continued urgently. He took out a large white handkerchief and mopped sweat from his brow and neck, even though the interior of the car was pleasantly cool, made so by efficient air-conditioning. *'Por Dios!'*

he exclaimed, losing his calmness suddenly. 'I've had a bad night thinking about you and about how we must have upset you. All of us, Janice and I, and Rafael too.' He turned to her with a pleading expression in his eyes. 'You won't take revenge on me for what has happened to you while you've been here, will you? Please, Glenda, say you won't.'

'Revenge? What do you mean? How could I take revenge on you?'

'I've been worried all night in case you took revenge by writing an article about me and Janice, criticising us, vilifying us,' he explained, wiping his brow again. 'You see, that is what she did,' he added in a mutter, looking out of the window beside him.

'Who did?' demanded Glenda, aware that the car had reached the end of the lane. It paused, then, since no vehicle was going past on the highway, it swung out, turning left. She sank back in relief. It was going in the direction of the turn-off to the airport. 'Who is "she"?' she persisted, opening her notebook and finding the page on which she had written the information Rafael had given her. Time was going by and the interview hadn't shown any signs of getting started yet. Somehow she must hurry César along, but first she wanted very much to find out who had written a critical, vilifying article about him.

'Paula Van Druten,' he said. 'You have heard of her, perhaps?' She shook her head negatively but wrote the name in her notebook.' She was our neighbour in New York,' he went on. 'She has plans to write a great novel. I was helping her with it, then Janice got jealous of Paula and wouldn't let her into our apartment. Wouldn't let me visit Paula either. *Dios,* what a situation!' he groaned. 'The worst I have ever found myself in. It was exactly how that English poet once described it. You remember?'

'William Congreve, you mean?' she suggested, trying hard to stifle her amusement at his predicament in New York. 'He wrote, "Heaven has no rage like love to hatred turned, Nor hell a fury like a woman scorned." Was it like that?'

'Exactly. I was caught between two furies.'

'And there was no twin brother around to help you out of the hole you had dug for yourself,' Glenda said drily.

César's head swung around. He stared at her. She couldn't see the expression in his eyes because of light reflected in the lenses of his glasses, but she had the impression he was surprised.

'Rafael told me, last night,' she explained. 'He told me how he has often pretended to be you when you have needed help. Now, please will you tell me what Paula Van Druten did to take revenge on you and then we'll get on with the interview.'

As if relieved by her calm matter-of-factness, César also sank back in his seat with a deep sigh.

'She wrote an article in which she made fun of Janice and me, exposing our private life for everyone to read about it. *Dios,* it was awful! I was afraid you might do something like that, so I have come to see you this morning, to apologise for what happened yesterday. You can interview me, Glenda, as long as you promise to write nothing about Janice or my marriage.'

'Since I know very little about Janice or your marriage it would be difficult for me to comment on either,' she replied coolly. 'I know only what Rafael has told me and that Janice knows I knew you in Montreal and she feared I might take advantage of that past friendship to start up an affair with you. Was he right?'

'Yes, he was right.' He sighed again. 'She did think that.'

'But surely you knew, or at least remembered, I wouldn't be like that!' Glenda exclaimed. 'Surely you realised I would never make any claims on you or be vindictive enough to take revenge on you for what happened yesterday.'

'I really know very little about you,' he replied defensively. 'It's true we went around in the same group in Montreal, but we were never alone together. Rafael got to know you better than I on those two visits he made.'

'Did he ever tell you I thought he was you when he turned up for the ski-trip to Quebec City?'

'Yes, he did.' His lips twitched in a slight mischievous smile that made him look more like his twin. 'We used to be much more alike than we are now. We used to play on our likeness, pretend to be each other.' The smile faded. 'We had fun in those days, he and I.' He sighed again and then added, 'He loves you, Glenda and yesterday he told me that of all the women he has ever met you're the only one he has ever wanted to marry. Did he ask you to marry him last night?'

'Yes, he did.' She look down at her notebook.
The words on the open page blurred.

'And?'

'I refused,' she said briskly, sitting up straight.
'Time is going on, and I would like to jot down
a few things. I have the information about where
you were born and educated, but I'd like to know
why you decided to go to university in Canada
to take your master's degree in English.'

'Oh, that's easy,' he replied. 'I knew some other
guys who had gone to study in Montreal. They
told me of the good time they had had there and
how it was less expensive to attend a university
there than to go to the States or to Britain. And
it offered all I wanted, a good grounding in the
greatest literature in the world.'

'You think English literature the greatest then?'

'Doesn't anyone who reads? More has been
written in English than in any other language.
And I wanted to write my novel in English
because I wanted it to reach certain people,
people who read only English and speak only
English but among whom Spanish-speaking
people have to live. Important people in govern-
ments and politics who have influence.'

'In the States,' she suggested, scribbling
furiously, her head bent. She was glad the ride in
the big car was smooth, the result of good shock-
absorbers and suspension.

'In all English-speaking countries,' he replied.
'Why did you refuse Rafael? Don't you like him?'

'I . . . Why do you want to know?' she
parried, and went on writing.

'Because I care about him and what happens

to him. We have always helped each other, he and I. Mostly he has helped me, because I seem to need more help than he does. He knows better how to deal with people than I do.' César laughed a little. 'As he says, I am the dreamer and he is the realist. Don't you like him?'

'Yes, I do.' Glenda spoke impatiently. 'Now back to your novel, please. We have only a few more minutes to discuss it. How long did it take you to write it?'

'I'm not sure. Many years. I am a slow thinker and it took me a long time to plot it, to create the characters.'

'Would you say it took you about eight years?'

'More than that. I had started to think about it before I went to Canada. It is a coalescence of my feelings and thoughts about my own people. You have read it?'

'I wouldn't have dared to interview you about it if I hadn't,' she replied.

'Good. I'm glad you have. I don't care for interviewers who haven't read the works of writers they are interviewing. What did you think of it?'

'I found it very sad.'

'We are a sad people, most of us brought to the western hemisphere by our Spanish masters and dumped on these islands or on the continent and then abandoned to our fate.' César spoke passionately, roused at last, and Glenda wrote fast, wishing she hadn't left her tape-recorder in Samana, unaware of where the car was going as she concentrated on César's answers to her many questions. To her delight, he talked at length about the problems he had encountered when writing his novel as well as his plans for the next book, and as he talked and she listened and scribbled she began to realise that he cared for his writing more than anything else in the world. He was truly an egocentric artist, putting his creative work first. His head was in the clouds. No wonder he wasn't any good at dealing with people and landed himself in difficult situations!

He stopped talking, and she finished her writing and looked out, noticing that the car was slowing down ready to stop. Through the window she saw not the airport terminal buildings, as she had expected, but another beach curving beside the sea. The car swung off the narrow coast road it was following and into a narrow lane between trees and shrubs, then bumped gently over a rough surface and into a courtyard in front of a long bungalow with a red-tiled roof.

'Oh! Where are we?' Glenda exclaimed, and glanced quickly at her watch. To her dismay the interview had taken longer than the half an hour she had expected. 'The plane will be taking off in thirty minutes. Tell your driver to go straight to the airport now and to step on it. I'll miss the plane!

'You have missed it,' replied César calmly, and for a moment it could have been Rafael speaking. 'Even if I asked Carlos to drive you to the airport now you wouldn't get there in time. We have come a long way past it—almost fifty miles. I intended to delay you long enough to miss the plane, and I have.'

'But why? I don't understand. Oh, you're as bad as Rafael with your tricks!' she fumed. 'What am I going to do now? How am I going to get back to Toronto? I was on a charter flight and it will be very difficult to change the ticket for one with a regular flight, besides costing me much more money, more than I have. And I'll have to stay another night or maybe two in a hotel. Oh, why have you done this, César? I can't afford to stay any longer.'

'You could afford to stay if you stayed with Rafael,' he replied imperturbably. 'And if you stayed he might not return to Nicaragua.' He sighed heavily and slanted her a curious glance. 'Did he tell you he would be going back there last night?'

'No. He's told me nothing about himself—or at least not much. How could he when most of the time he was pretending to be you,' said Glenda in a low shaken voice. 'Why, why does he want to go back to Central America?'

'To continue with the work he has been doing there for the past three years as a volunteer doctor. He was first in El Salvador and then in Nicaragua, treating the civilian population suffering from the effects of civil war, going from village to village on foot, his medical supplies strapped on his back. Then a few months ago he was hit by a stray bullet from a guerilla's gun and had to be treated himself. He came home to recover and has been working again with our people here. We need doctors like him here and he would stay, I think, if he were married and had a family of his own.' César paused and gave another of his deep sighs. 'He told me he was going to ask you to marry him last night—we tell each other everything when we are together. And I hoped that you would accept his proposal. I would like to know, Glenda, why you refused.'

'He . . . he asked me too soon after I'd found out how he'd pretended to be you,' she replied. 'César, you must see how hard it would be for me to trust him after what he's done.'

'I can see that, yes,' he said. 'Then you don't love him?'

'Yes, I do. More than anyone,' she admitted forlornly. 'I . . . I fell in love with him eight years ago, but I thought he was you. When I met him again, the other day, I realised I was still in love with him and he told me he loved me. I hoped he would ask me to stay and live with him, even offer to marry me because he told me . . . as you . . . that his marriage was over. Then I found out the man I had been loving wasn't the person I'd believed him to be.'

'Yes, he was,' César argued. 'He was himself, not me. He was just using my name. I've never loved or wanted you, Glenda. He has. He still does. But you don't love him. If you did, you'd forgive his deception of you. After all, what's in a name? It's feelings that matter.'

'Did he ask you to delay me like this?' she asked, her head bent as she doodled on her notebook. Her mind was in turmoil again.

'No, he didn't. It was my own idea. As I've told you, I had a bad night of it, thinking about you and about him. I had a strong feeling you might refuse him because you felt he had deceived you and I had to do something about it, something to repay him for all the help he has given me over the years. He is reckless, cares nothing for what danger he might step into if he returns to Central America, thinks only of helping others less privileged than he has been. But we care, my parents and I. And I'd hoped you would care too, Glenda.'

'I do, I do,' she muttered. 'I care very much. But he didn't seem to mind when I refused, and he didn't persist.'

'Nor will he. He's too proud. The next move is yours, if you care enough to make it. And now, since you've missed that plane, you have the chance. Do you want to take it?'

'How? What can I do?' She looked up at him.

'I'm going to leave you here to visit a friend of mine who lives in this house. Carlos will drive you to Samana if you wish.' César glanced at his watch. 'You might get there in time.'

'In time for what?'

'To stop him from making plans to fly out of the country today. I know that's what he had planned to do if you refused his proposal. Shall I tell Carlos to take you there?'

With the air-conditioning off, the interior of the car was growing very warm. Sunlight was slanting in the window beside Glenda, seeming to sear the skin on the back of her neck. Errant thoughts tumbled about her mind. She thought of the plane that had taken off for Canada so recently, of her luggage. Had it gone on the plane or had it been left at the airport? She thought of Ida's taunt when she had left her. She thought of Rafael's whispered *adiós* that morning when he had left her. She thought of Rafael. He loomed larger and larger in her thoughts until he had taken over completely and she succumbed to the longing she felt to see him again, to be with him . . .

'Yes,' she whispered. 'Please tell Carlos to drive me to Samana.'

With his slow smile, so like and yet so unlike Rafael's smile, César leaned forward and kissed her on the cheek.

'Bueno,' he murmured. 'I wish you much luck, Glenda, and I hope you succeed. If you are successful I shall look forward to seeing both of you tomorrow. If you are not, come back to Puerto Plata to my house. You can stay there until you have made arrangements to fly to Canada. *Adiós,* for now.'

He leaned forward to give instructions to Carlos, then got out of the car and shut the door. Immediately the engine started up and the car was reversed. Glenda had time to wave to César before the car shot forward along the lane back to the shore road.

She leaned back and closed her eyes. She found her heart was thumping far faster than usual. She felt both excited and disconcerted. In a little more than sixty minutes her life had been reversed like a vehicle. Now, instead of going to catch a plane to fly to Canada, she was going to Samana again to see Rafael. Yet if César hadn't come to see her this morning she would have been high in the sky by now, returning to Canada with nothing, nothing but a bittersweet memory of seduction by a man she loved dearly and whom she would have agreed to marry if he hadn't tricked her.

She opened her eyes and sat up abruptly, her notebook sliding off her knees to the floor. Rafael didn't deserve that she should go to Samana to see him. He had tricked her, seduced her, she argued. Oh, never mind that she had been willing and had known exactly what she had been doing and had wanted to do it with him; the fact remained that he hadn't told her he wasn't César. He had deceived her.

And she had let him.

She couldn't get away from that fact either. Nor could she explain satisfactorily to herself her behaviour of last night. After refusing to marry him she had quite happily let him make love to her. Why? Because she loved him and wanted him. Because she wanted to be his mate, his mistress, his wife, more than anything else in the world.

She wished he had told her about his years in Central America. The knowledge that he had worked voluntarily to heal the sick and tend the dying put him in a new light. He wasn't merely a wealthy playboy playing tricks on unsuspecting women. He was a strongwilled, free-thinking adult, compassionate and practical, and he had told his twin brother that he loved her and that she was the only woman he had ever wanted to marry.

The car swerved out on to the highway again, turning left. She leaned forward to speak to Carlos.

'How far to Samana?' she asked.

'We keep going at this speed we be there pretty soon, in another hour. No problem,' he replied, and flashed her a grin over his shoulder.

Glenda sat back again. After her initial annoy-
ance at realising that once again she had been
tricked by an Estrada, this time by César, into
missing her flight back to Canada, she felt a
strong urge to laugh. She had been kidnapped by
him in the gentlest possible way. By keeping her
busy writing down his answers, César had
prevented her from noticing how fast the car was
travelling in an easterly direction and she had
been so interested in all he had been saying that
she had been oblivious to the passage of time
too. In his own way he was as clever a deceiver
as Rafael.

On and on the big car purred, past the plantations of coconut palms and small shacks, past
the village where the road through the hills joined
the highway, on and on and into the town of
Sanchez, through it and along the coast of the
wide bay of Samana, hazy today under the hot
sunshine, with no view of distant mountains. Up
a hill and down again, past the shopping centre
and the market to turn on the wide boulevard.
White rectangles of buildings gleamed against
tropical foliage. Blue water shimmered. Yachts
swung to anchor chains. Flags fluttered idly in
the light breeze.

Was it only at this time yesterday she had
boarded the *público* for Puerto Plata? Glenda
wondered as the car passed the wharf. The area
was crowded with people, local people on holiday
waiting to board the ferry that would take them
to the island of Sabana de la Mar. Then the car
was past and speeding away from the town, up

the curving road that mounted the cliffs.

Half hidden by trees and shrubs the walls of Rafael's hideaway shone yellow in the sunlight. The big car crunched to a stop in the parking space. Excitement pulsed through Glenda at the thought of surprising Rafael. What would he say? What would he say? What would he do? But what was more to the point, what was she going to say to him? How was she going to explain her unexpected, uninvited arrival at his house when she was supposed to be on her way back to Toronto?

As she stepped out of the big grey car she noticed that the Hyundai truck was parked in its usual place. Beside it was another car, a small black one. Rosario's car? Was the young woman in the house at this moment comforting Rafael? Jealousy scorched through Glenda and she almost got back into the grey car and ordered Carlos to take her back to Puerto Plata. She wasn't going to stoop to fighting with another woman for Rafael. No matter how much she loved him, she refused to compete.

'Carlos, please wait,' she said. 'I think I might be going back to Puerto Plata. I just have to go into the house to get something while I'm here.'

He didn't reply, just nodded agreeably. She closed the car door and, squaring her shoulders proudly and gritting her teeth, she marched up the wrought-iron staircase that led up to the veranda.

She turned on to the veranda. Someone was coming in a blind rush the other way, a slim black-haired woman who was wearing a gaudily coloured dress.

'You? What are you doing here?' exclaimed Rosario, pulling up short. She had obviously been crying stormily and was in fact still heaving with sobs. Her mascara had run again to streak her cheeks. Glenda lifted her head proudly.

'I've come back to get my tape-recorder,' she announced coldly.

CHAPTER TEN

ONE hand at her heaving breasts, the gold chain around her neck glittering, Rosario stepped back a pace, her black-ringed, tear-smudged eyes wide and staring.

'I don't believe you,' she retorted tauntingly with a little toss of her head.

'But it's true. I have come for it. I left it here yesterday and I can't leave without it,' said Glenda stubbornly. Not for anything was she going to admit that she had come only to see Rafael.

'But yesterday you said you would be leaving for Canada this morning,' argued Rosario, who was fast recovering her normal fierceness.

'I know I did, but just as I was going to the airport I remembered the tape-recorder, so I came here to get it,' insisted Glenda. Soon she would be believing her own argument, she thought mockingly.

'Rafael thinks you have gone. He's told me you have left,' persisted Rosario, wiping away the few tears that remained on her cheeks with the back of one hand. With her rouged cheeks and her smudged eyes she looked for all the world like a clown.' He's leaving too. He going back to Nicaragua, this afternoon. I've tried to stop him from going. I offered to marry him if he would stay here and work here, even if he work among the poor people for ever. But he won't listen to me. He laugh at me. He tell me to go and marry Pedro instead.'

'So why don't you?' said Glenda gently. Surprisingly, the sharp feeling of jealously was fading. No longer did she see Rosario as a sort of *femme fatale,* a dark seductress intent on enticing Rafael to be her lover. She saw her clearly as she was, young and a little mixed-up, not sure what it was that she wanted from life.

'You think I should?' Rosario's eyebrows shot up in surprise. 'But you don't know Pedro. He never look at me except when we are dancing, and when we are not dancing or practising he go off with the other guys. He not stay with me.'

'Perhaps he thinks you're not interested in him except as a dancer,' suggested Glenda. 'Perhaps he believes you don't see him as a person with feelings and thoughts besides dancing. I think you should take Rafael's advice and start taking more interest in Pedro. It's possible that Rafael knows Pedro likes you as a person as well as a dancer, isn't it?'

'I guess so,' muttered Rosario, scowling. Then suddenly and swiftly she smiled, her whole face lighting up. 'I'll go—right now. I'll go and find Pedro and tell him that after all I prefer to marry him and not Rafael.' She flashed a vindictive glance at the open glass doorway and flinging back her head shouted loudly in Spanish. Glenda only caught a little of what the other woman shouted. It seemed that Rosario was informing Rafael that she had no intention of waiting any longer for him to marry her. She wasn't going to wait until her hair was grey and he was in a wheelchair.

'There,' she said when she finished shouting, and she smiled winningly at Glenda. 'I feel much better now. You can have him. Me, I wouldn't have him now if he came begging me on his knees. You are welcome to him. *Adiós*, Glenda.'

Rosario skipped away along the veranda and disappeared down the steps. For a few moments Glenda lingered on the veranda, amused by Rosario's behaviour. She heard the roar of the little black car's engine as it started up. Wheels crunched on gravel. The sound of the engine faded as it went up the hill and all was silent. No birds whistled and no monkeys chattered in the midday heat. The sunshine poured down from the sky and she was glad of the shade on the veranda.

She half expected Rafael to appear in the open doorway to make some sort of stinging retort to Rosario's last taunt, but he didn't. The minutes crawled by while she hesitated, hot, heavy and drowsy, her pride at war with her instincts. Pride suggested that she should turn and leave now before Rafael appeared, before she had to face him and explain why she hadn't gone to Canada that morning but was there instead, while instinct was urging her to reject pride's arguments and enter the house; to be like Rosario and lay bare her heart, show him she felt about him.

Slowly she turned and moved towards the doorway, and looked into the living-room. It looked the same as it had yesterday, and no one was in it. She stepped inside and paused, listening for sounds of movement that would betray to her the whereabouts of Rafael. She heard only the sound of water dripping from a tap in the kitchen.'

Crossing the living-room, she went into the kitchen. Rafael wasn't there, but her tape-recorder was on the table. There was an envelope and some writing paper beside it, as if someone had been about to write a note and prepare the recorder for mailing. The piece of paper on which she had written her address for Alberto was also on the table. She picked up the recorder and turned back to the doorway. Shock shivered through her and she let out an exclamation of surprise. Rafael was standing in the doorway watching her.

'Oh, what a scare you gave me!' she gasped. 'Why didn't you make some noise to let me know you were coming into the room?'

'So why didn't you call out and let me know you were in the house?' he retorted coolly, 'instead of creeping about as if you didn't want to be heard.' He leaned one shoulder against the jamb of the doorway and pushed his hands into the pockets of his white shorts. His crossed feet were bare, his hair was tousled, his eyes were dark, ringed with tired lines. All the sparkle in him, the brightness, seemed to have been doused. 'What are you doing here?' he asked. 'I thought you'd have left by now. Your flight must have taken off over an hour ago.'

'I . . . I . . . ' Glenda looked down at the recorder in her hand. Pride was very difficult to overcome in the face of his weary coolness. 'I

remembered I'd left this here, so I came for it.'
she said, and managed to sound cool too.

'You missed your flight just to come back for
that?' Scorn rasped in his voice and she looked
up at him quickly. 'Why? There's nothing on the
tape that is in it.'

'How do you know?' she demanded.

'I played it to make sure you hadn't taped
anything I'd said to you the other evening.'

'You mean when you were pretending to be
César?' she queried, meeting scorn with scorn.

'When you still believed I was César,' he
retorted. 'Or were pretending you believed I was
César.'

'I wasn't pretending,' she began hotly, and
broke off. 'Oh, what's the use?' she sighed. 'It
will always be there between us, the fact that you
let me go on thinking you were him. You deceived
me.'

'Only about my name, never about how I felt
about you and still feel about you,' he said
quietly.

Unable to look at him in case she gave in to
an impulse to fling her arms about him, a little
intimidated by his coolness, Glenda looked down
again at the tape-recorder in her hand.

'How did you come here this morning?' he
asked.

'By car. It's waiting to take me back.' Why
was it they were both so stiff? Why couldn't she
find the words to tell him she made a mistake
when she had refused his proposal last night, that
she loved him and wanted to live with him, would

marry him, would do anything to stop him going back to Central America?

He stepped over to the window that overlooked the parking space and looked out.

'What sort of car?' he asked.

'A big grey one. I'm not sure of the make.'

'It isn't there,' he said curtly.

'It must be.' She went over to his side to peer out of the window too. Only the Hyundai truck was in its place under the casuarina trees. Glaringly bright in the strong sunlight, the rest of the parking area was empty. 'He . . . the driver, Carlos must have gone to park in the shade somewhere, up the lane perhaps,' she said uncertainly. 'I'll go and look.'

Turning, she hurried across the kitchen into the living-room and across to the open patio door. She almost ran along the veranda to the steps and down them. Standing on the sunbaked gravel, she peered up the tree-shaded lane. There was no car parked in the shade of the trees; Carlos had driven it away. Once again she was stranded and dependent upon Rafael for transport. She had no doubts that César had given instructions to Carlos to leave as soon as he had deposited her at Rafael's house.

Pushing the tape-recorder into her handbag, she turned back to the steps and slowly mounted them. The run to find the car seemed to have sapped her energy and the midday heat was making her feel drowsy. She longed to lie down somewhere and sleep. No wonder the Spanish-speaking peoples enjoyed their *siesta!* But how could she rest when she had still to break through

Rafael's new and surprising reserve? César had been right when he had told her his brother was proud. And she was so lacking in confidence when it came to dealing with this sort of situation; she had a tendency to withdraw herself behind the barrier of her pride when confronted with coolness and uninterest.

As she turned on the veranda a movement at the other end of it drew her attention. The hammock in which she had slept with Rafael the previous night was swinging gently. Rafael was asprawl in it, one sinewy bare leg and foot hanging over the side. She walked the length of the veranda, her heart beating loudly in her ears, and stood at the side of the hammock to look down at him. Under the dishevelled sand-coloured hair his brow was smooth, save for two deeply carved thought lines. His eyes were closed, black lashes fan-like. The firm line of his lips was slightly relaxed. He looked as if he were asleep already, within a few minutes of having lain down.

'Rafael,' she murmured. She wished she could have lain on the hammock beside him but couldn't think of a way to get on it.

'Mmm?' He raised his eyelids slightly, looked at her through his lashes. 'You still here?' he drawled.

'The car's gone,' she said with a touch of impatience. 'César must have told Carlos to return to Puerto Plata after he had left me here.'

His eyes opened fully and he frowned.

'César sent you here?' he asked.

'He didn't send me. He just made it possible

for me to come if I wanted to come,' she said
defensively. 'He came to the hotel this morning
to apologise for yesterday afternoon and to let
me interview him, in the car. He promised to
take me to the airport to catch the plane, but by
the time I . . . we . . . had finished talking it
was too late. He . . . he said Carlos would
drive me here if . . . if I wanted to come.' The
way he was looking at her, his eyes as bright and
sharp as an eagle's was destroying her poise. She
felt a desire to turn and run away from him
because he looked so scornfully sceptical of her
explanation.

'And did you want to come?' he asked, settling
back against the cushions and closing his eyes
again, as if he'd lost interest.

'Or course. I wanted to get my tape-recorder,'
she said weakly.

His eyes opened again. He sat up suddenly and
the hammock rocked violently. Reaching out a
hand, he snatched her bag from her and flung it
as far as he could over the veranda rail. The bag
disappeared into the thickness of the shrubbery
where the microphone of the tape-recorder had
disappeared two nights ago.

'Oh, why did you do that?' Glenda exclaimed
furiously.

Sliding off the hammock, Rafael stood over
her, eyes alight with anger, lips curling sardonically.

'Was the tape-recorder all you came for?' he
demanded, his voice rasping. 'If so, go and get it
and then clear out. I don't want you here if you
can't be more honest.'

'I am honest. Everything I've just told you is
the truth. César did come to the hotel and he did
make me miss the plane and suggested . . . '
She broke off, realising suddenly that what she
had been going to say might make him angrier
than ever.

'And he suggested you came here,' he guessed,
his voice crackling icily. 'You didn't come here
of your own volition, because you wanted to,
then. You came because he sent you here. Right?'

'Yes. But I wanted to come too, to . . . '

'To get your tape-recorder,' he interrupted
tautly.

'No, not just for that.' Frustration because he
was deliberately misunderstanding her, combined
with disappointment because he wasn't more
welcoming, boiled up in her. She felt her head
might burst at any minute. It wasn't a good time
of day, she realised, to have a reasonable discussion about anything. It was too hot for reason,
so why let reason prevail? Why not let passion
take over? She loved him, didn't she? And had
been told he loved her not only by himself but
also by his brother. So why hesitate any more?'

She looked straight ahead at the strong brown
column of his neck rising up from the open collar
of his shirt and felt desire swell and burst within
her. All reason fled before the emotion that
poured through her. Her fingers touched his
throat before she told them to and she lifted her
face to his and whispered,

'I came because I love you and I couldn't bear
the thought of going away from you. I was going
to tell you last night, but you fell asleep before I

could, and this morning when I woke up you had gone.'

She wasn't allowed to say any more. His arms went around her and his lips claimed hers fiercely and hungrily. Her hands slid round to the nape of his neck, curled in the tough strands of his hair. Under her blouse, his hands slipped in a searching caress. Then, his lips leaving hers, he lifted her easily and, laying her on the hammock, climbed in beside her. As it rocked wildly they clung to each other face to face, stifling their laughter with kisses.

Gradually the hammock stopped swinging violently. All was silent and still, the air soft and warm, drenched with sunlight beyond the shade of the veranda. Everything—the birds, the monkeys, the trees, the usually perpetual trade-wind breeze—seemed to be taking a *siesta*.

Lying with Rafael in intimate embrace, Glenda at last felt all her inhibitions sliding away from her. Pride had been overcome by instinct.

'I met Rosario when I arrived,' she murmured, arching her throat to the exploring touch of his lips and inhaling the scent of his hair as it brushed against her face. 'She told me you intend to leave for Nicaragua today.'

'I have now missed the plane,' he said. 'You made sure I would miss it just by coming here, in the same way César made sure you missed your flight to Canada this morning, something I'll always be grateful to him for. I thought you'd gone and that I would never see you again.'

There was silence for a while while they kissed passionately, their mouths clinging in open possessiveness, their fingers busy too, sliding under the edges of clothing, stroking, titillating vulnerable hollows and nerve-endings.

'Did you mean what you said a few moments ago about not being able to bear the thought of going away from me?' Rafael murmured drowsily.

'Yes, I did. I'm glad César was able to detain me, too,' she whispered. His head was heavy against her breast, his lips warm against her bare skin, flickering, tantalising, sending all sorts of exciting sensations tingling through her. 'You see, I . . . I'd realised I do want to be married to you after all,' she confessed.

'But last night in the restaurant you said you couldn't marry me because you didn't trust me,' he said, raising his head sharply and looking at her, his eyes bright with suspicion. 'You said you couldn't forgive me for pretending to be César.'

'I know I did. I . . . I changed my mind.' She raised a hand to stroke his cheek. 'Last night in the restaurant I was too confused after finding out that all these years it was you I've been remembering and not a man called César. You asked me to marry you too soon, before I'd had time to come to terms with the idea.'

'That was because I thought I had so little time,' he admitted. 'You were so set on going back to Canada today. But we'll not think of that any more. That's over. You can go back to Canada after we're married, and I can go to Nicaragua.'

'But . . . but . . .' Astounded by this

announcement, Glenda stared up him in puzzlement.

'But what?' he asked, lips slanting in a smile as he leaned over her and stroked her hair. 'Still not trusting me, *querida?* You should. I don't often make promises, but when I do I keep them, you can be very sure of that. Ask César. Ask anyone who knows me.'

'I want to trust you,' she whispered. 'It's just that I don't understand why you want to go back to Nicaragua after we're married. César said this morning that you might not want to go back there once you were married.'

'So now, at last, we get at the whole truth,' he drawled, his face hardening. 'You didn't come here because you love me. You came to stop me from going back to Nicaragua, because César asked you to. You were quite happy to join him in a conspiracy to prevent me from leaving this country.' He flung himself away from her and rolled off the hammock. Standing beside it, he looked down at her contemptuously. 'Who is deceiving whom now?' he rasped.

'I'm not deceiving you!' she retorted hotly, sitting up sharply so that the hammock rocked. 'I've come because I love you and would like to marry you. But I don't see much point in us getting married if you're going to go off to the jungles of Central America immediately after the ceremony.'

'You'd expect me to stay with you, eh? You'd expect me to go to Canada with you? I see.' Hands on his, hips he glared down at her 'You're no better than any other woman. No better than

Janice or Rosario. You want to trap a man, tie him down at your side all the time.' He raked a hand through his hair. 'So be it. We'll forget all about being married, then.' He glanced at his wristwatch. 'There's no way I can catch the plane I intended to catch, but if I leave right away I might get on another flying to Cuba today and from there I might be able to hop over to Managua somehow,' he muttered.

Turning on his heel, he strode away and into the house. Bewildered by his change-about, Glenda wrestled with her pride again and came to a conclusion. Scrambling off the hammock, she followed him and found him in the bedroom where he was finishing packing a rucksack.

'I'm not like Janice. Or Rosario,' she asserted, her outrage at being sneered at by him making her breathless. 'And you know I'm not. I love you and I'd like to marry you, that's why I'm here. It . . . it's hard for me to make that commitment to you. My first marriage was a disaster . . . ' Her voice faltered and she couldn't go on.

Rafael looked up from what he was doing and straight at her. Letting go of the rucksack, he came over to her and put his arms around her to hold her closely.

'I know. I understand,' he murmured. He pushed her away from him a little so that he could see her face properly. 'And I guess I should have been more honest with you, told you more about myself before proposing to you. But I want you so much to be my wife and I've been so afraid I would lose you that I've tended to act too impetuously. I should have told you that marriage, even to you whom I love more than any other woman I have known, won't stop me doing what I feel in my guts I have to do. It won't stop me going back to Nicaragua.'

His expression was very serious and, seeing him clearly as if for the first time, her view unblurred by romantic feelings or by anger, Glenda noted the determined set of his jaw and wondered what had made her believe he would ever be deterred from a course of action he had planned for himself by marriage to her or any other woman. Yet she felt she had to try and deter him.

'But it's so dangerous,' she whispered, sliding a hand up his chest, her fingers slipping inside the opening of his shirt. 'César told me this morning that you were wounded, and I noticed the first night we made love, when we were in the shower, the place high up on your shoulder where the bullet must have entered. If . . . if you go back you might be killed.'

'That's no reason for not going. Would you have me be a coward?' He shrugged. 'I could just as easily be killed here, or anywhere else, crossing the street. Do you want to change your mind and not marry me? I promised I would go back, to see the people I tried to help. To see if they survived the treatment I gave them.' His slanted smile mocked himself. 'I have to go to tie up loose ends, but if you agree to marry me here, during the next few days, I won't leave until after we have had a short honeymoon.'

'But what will I do after you've gone?'

'You can go back to Canada, if you wish. I'm
sure you have a few loose ends to tie up too. You
have an article to write about César, perhaps
other projects to finish. And I have no objection
to you continuing with your career.' His smile
widened tauntingly. 'Could be you'll be so busy
during the next few months awaiting the birth of
our child you'll never think of me!'

'A child?' she exclaimed, a hand going involuntarily to her abdomen. The thought of conceiving
had never entered her mind before. Now it filled
her with a sort of pleasurable panic. 'What makes
you think we're going to have a child?' she
challenged him.

'After the way we've been behaving during the
past fews days there's every possibility of it,' he
retorted, laughing at her. 'And about time, too,
for you to have a baby, for you to be a mother
and for me to be a father. Neither of us is getting
any younger.' Devilry was back in his eyes,
glinting at her as he drew her closer to him.
Above hers his lips quirked tormentingly. 'So
what now? Do you change your mind again? Will
you marry me now?'

'Is the possibility that I might have your child
the only reason you have asked me to marry
you?' she riposted, leaning back against his arms.

'Not the only reason, no. I want to marry you
to make sure you're mine for ever to come home
to, for the reasons all other men want to marry.
I want to make sure that we're going to have a
future together when I've done what I have to
do. But I would prefer any child of mine to be
born in wedlock, to have two parents and not a

single parent. Do you still want to marry me?'

'I don't seem to have any other alternative open to me,' Glenda teased him lightly. 'You see, I love you and I want you—to come home to me always. I want you to be there when our child is born. Will you promise you'll be there?'

'I promise,' he said, and kissed her hard on the lips. The packing of the rucksack was forgotten as once more she succumbed to the sweet seduction of his lovemaking and they convinced each other that they loved each other. There was no more talk for a while, no mention of planes to be caught or loose ends to be tied up. *Siesta* that afternoon was long after they had satisfied the demands of passion.

They were married a few days later in a quiet ceremony attended by César, Janice and their children as well as Rafael's and César's parents; cables were to Glenda's parents and to Ida informing them of the marriage. The following seven days were spent by Glenda and Rafael in blissful seclusion at his hideaway in Samana. Although disappointed by Rafael's decision to return to Nicaragua, César was at the airport to see him off and also to see Glenda depart for Toronto.

During the next few months, Glenda saw the publication of her articles about César and the Dominican Republic and received more commissions to write. She was busy, very involved with her writing. But she missed Rafael desperately in a way she had never missed anyone in her life before, and she was delighted when she was at last able to write to him to tell him she was expecting their child. Now she was sure he would come to her. He had promised he would and he never broke a promise.

As it turned out, he was late. Delayed by bad weather and cancelled flights, he arrived on a cold day in January twenty-four hours after the baby boy had been born.

His skin burned dark by hot suns, his strange hair cropped short, he came to where she lay in the pristine whiteness of the hospital bed, the baby asleep in a crib beside her.

'I couldn't manage twins,' Glenda joked lightly, covering up, as always, the surge of deep emotion that rushed through her on seeing him again.

'I'm glad you couldn't. They would have always been pretending to be each other and confusing you,' he retorted with his slanted smile. 'Have you missed me?'

'More than I can ever tell you,' she whispered. 'Have you missed me?'

'So much that it will be a long time before I leave you again,' he said, lifting one of her hands to kiss it, his eyes burning with an amber light.

'Does that mean you're not going back there?' she asked hopefully.

'It does. I've done what I had to do and I'm ready now to work in my own country. But only if you will come with me, Glenda. Will you come back to Samana with me as soon as you and the child are ready to travel?'

Samana. A tropical paradise. Sunlight, whispering palms, a turquoise sea.

'We'll be ready soon,' she said, simply and happily. 'We'll go with you anywhere. I love you.'

'And I you,' he murmured deeply.

And as she received his quick passionate kiss it seemed to Glenda she saw their future together stretching before her like an endless beach of golden sand, bright with promises that had been made and would be kept by both of them.

Harlequin Intrigue
Adopts a New Cover Story!

We are proud to present to you the new Harlequin Intrigue cover design.

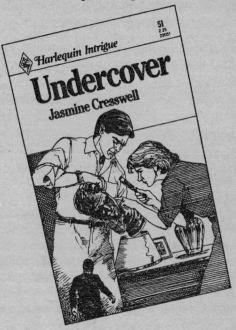

Look for two exciting new stories each month, which mix a contemporary, sophisticated romance with the surprising twists and turns of a puzzler . . . romance with "something more."

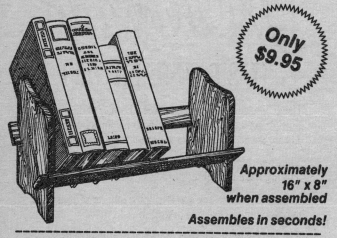

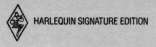

JUST ONE NIGHT

Hawk Sinclair—Texas millionaire and owner of the exclusive
Sinclair hotels, determined to protect his son's inheritance.
Leonie Spencer—desperate to protect her sister's happiness.

They were together for just one night.
The night their daughter was conceived.

Blackmail, kidnapping and attempted murder add suspense
to passion in this exciting bestseller.

The success story of Carole Mortimer continues with *Just
One Night*, a captivating romance from the author of the
bestselling novels, *Gypsy* and *Merlyn's Magic*.

★

**Available in March
wherever paperbacks are sold.**